Fireweed

Fireweed

Mickey Minner

P.D. Publishing, Inc.
Clayton, North Carolina

Copyright © 2009 by Mickey Minner

All rights reserved. No part of this publication may be reproduced, transmitted in any form or by any means, electronic or mechanical, including photocopy, recording, or any information storage and retrieval system, without permission in writing from the publisher. The characters herein are fictional and any resemblance to a real person, living or dead, is purely coincidental. Any resemblance to actual events, locales, or organizations is entirely coincidental and beyond the intent of the author.

ISBN-13: 978-1-933720-59-3
ISBN-10: 1-933720-59-X

9 8 7 6 5 4 3 2 1

Cover photo by Mickey Minner
Cover design by Barb Coles
Edited by: Day Petersen/Medora MacDougall

Published by:

P.D. Publishing, Inc.
P.O. Box 70
Clayton, NC 27528

http://www.pdpublishing.com

Acknowledgements

I would like to thank the readers who take time from their busy lives to read my stories and write me with words of encouragement. And the members of my discussion group who generously support my writing yet keep my feet firmly rooted to the ground.

I would also like to thank Linda and Barb at PD Publishing for their enthusiastic support of my writing; Day Petersen, Medora MacDougall for their editing expertise and guiding me through the process; and Jo Fothergill for her unending support.

The Sweetwater Saga stories are dedicated to my Grandfather, Charley F. Stetler, who inspired my love for the old west — a love that has never faded and continues to deepen. And to my Grandmother, Edith M. Stetler, who always said I should be a writer. To my parents, Bob and Madelyn Minner, who even when they didn't understand never stopped loving me.

CHAPTER ONE

Jesse Branson stood midway up the ladder, tightening the last of the bolts that secured two chains to a support beam of the porch roof. She tugged on the links to assure herself they would support the weight of the swing hanging below. Satisfied that the surprise for her wife was ready, Jesse climbed down and took a step back to view the results of her labors. Imagining Jennifer's reaction at seeing the swing, she smiled as she bent down to place her wrench back into her toolbox.

"Mommy." KC stomped purposefully toward the porch, stopping only when she reached the bottom step. She wasn't allowed to climb stairs by herself, and she knew all too well how unhappy her mother would be if she tried. "Mommy!" she persisted.

Her daughter's insistent calls broke into her thoughts, and Jesse straightened up to examine the mud-covered toddler with a critical but twinkling eye. "Yes, Sunshine?"

"Cha-wie bein' bad." KC wrinkled her nose. A piece of drying mud was making it itch, and she swiped at it with a muddy hand.

"Oh?" Jesse shifted her eyes from her daughter to look at her son sitting in the middle of a mud puddle a few feet away. "What's he doin'?" she asked as Charley happily slapped at the mud encircling him.

KC scowled. "He makin' mud pies."

"Well..." Jesse gave her daughter's statement due consideration. "Aren't you making mud pies, too?"

"Yep." KC's head bobbed up and down.

"So, why is Charley being bad if he's making mud pies?"

"He oosing my mud," KC said indignantly, stomping a bare foot into the sloppy ground to emphasize her objection.

Struggling to keep a smile off her face, Jesse scratched the back of her head as she surveyed the ranch yard. The melting winter snows and spring rains had turned most of the ground into a gooey mess. "I'm pretty sure there's enough mud in the yard for both of you, so, go back and share it with your brother."

KC frowned, studying her mother for a moment before twisting her head to look back over her shoulder at Charley playing without her. She sighed heavily. "Okay." She stomped back to her brother and the contested mud puddle.

Jesse chuckled and bent down to retrieve her toolbox. "I surely better get those two cleaned up before Jennifer gets home," she told herself as she straightened up.

"You want me to heat water for a bath, or shall we just dump them into the horse trough?"

Jesse turned and saw her mother standing on the other side of the screen door that led into the kitchen. "Hi, Mom. Didn't know you were inside."

"I needed some flour." Marie Branson pushed the screen door open and stepped out onto the porch. She and her husband had their own cabin on their daughter's ranch but were free to make use of the larger ranch house's accommodations, including the well-stocked kitchen. She laughed as KC plopped down beside her brother. "You sure got your hands full with that little one."

"Yep." Jesse took hold of the ladder, preparing to carry it and her toolbox back to the barn.

"You finished with the swing?"

"Yep. Hope Jennifer likes it as much as I think she will."

Marie walked over and gave the swing a gentle push. "I think she'll like it just fine." She turned back to face Jesse, who smiled. "So, about that bath?"

Jesse looked at the children and chuckled. Her daughter, who just moments before had been upset with her brother, was playing with the baby and giggling loudly as she diligently patted mud into flattened round shapes and passed them to Charley, who immediately threw them down, causing mud to splatter both children. "Better start the water heating. Dusty and Boy would never forgive me if I dunked them rascals in their trough."

Marie smiled. "I'll get the buckets ready."

"Thanks. I'll be back soon as I get these put away in the barn." Jesse stepped off the porch carrying the ladder and toolbox. "Sure be glad when this muck starts to dry out."

"Young 'uns won't." Marie turned to go back inside the house.

"They'll adjust," Jesse muttered, her boots sinking into the mud as she made her way across the soft ground.

Jennifer Branson watched her students file out of the schoolhouse, another day of lessons finished. She gathered up the papers spread about her desk and shuffled them into a neat pile before tucking them away in the desk drawer. Pushing up from the chair, she took a moment to stretch her aching back before reaching for her cane. It had been two years since she'd been attacked by a mountain lion. Her leg had healed as much as it was going to, and she depended on the cane, especially at the end of a long day. She limped to the row of coat hooks near the door of the schoolhouse. She was surprised to hear the sound of someone climbing the steps outside. She smiled, wondering if Jesse had come to pick her up.

"Jennifer?" A deep voice reverberated through the quiet room.

"In here, Ed," Jennifer called out to the storekeeper, a gentle giant of a man who had become her surrogate father during her time in Sweetwater.

Ed Granger entered the room, standing in the doorway for a moment while his eyes adjusted to coming in from the bright sunshine. "I was hoping I'd catch you. Stage brought you a letter." Ed rented a section of his store to the stage company and accepted all mail pouches. Since Sweetwater lacked an official post office, he also provided delivery service, sending the mail out with any freight deliveries to the ranches and mining camps. He usually held any letters and packages for the folks living in town to pick up, but Jennifer was special to him. "Thought I'd stretch my legs and bring this over before you left for the ranch."

"Thanks. I appreciate you taking the time to walk over." Jennifer accepted the envelope and then gave Ed a hug.

"Aren't you going to open it?" he asked when she shoved it into her coat pocket without even a casual glance.

"No. It's probably just another letter from Mother asking when we plan to travel East. It can wait until after I get back to Jesse and the children."

"Thinking of going back for a visit, are you?"

"To be honest, I really haven't given it much thought," Jennifer replied. "I know Mother would love for us to come, but I simply don't find the prospect very pleasing."

Ed nodded. Jennifer had told him of her childhood sharing a house with a father who thought of his daughter as nothing more than a pawn to further his business interests and three brothers who were too busy to spare a moment for her. Even though her father was now confined to a mental hospital and Jennifer had made peace with her brothers, Ed could understand her reluctance to return to the town of her birth and its unhappy memories.

Jennifer giggled as she led Ed through the doorway to the small porch at the front of the schoolhouse. "And can you imagine Jesse once we got there? She's used to wide open spaces. With all the buildings and the clamor of people and buggies in the streets, it wouldn't be but a day or two before she was feeling we'd been there long enough."

Pulling the door shut behind them, Ed laughed. "That would be a sight: Jesse in one of those crowded and noisy cities back East. Why, she hates to spend a full day in Sweetwater."

"And let's not forget about KC and Charley," Jennifer added with a smile. "I'm pretty sure that even with my three brothers keeping a tight hold on their reins, those two children could get into more trouble than the good citizens would be willing to tolerate."

"Ain't that the truth?"

Jennifer laughed. "Yes, I think it's best I keep my wild horses in the West, where they can run free."

Ed followed Jennifer down the stairs, then fell into step beside her as they walked along the gravel path to where her horse, Blaze, was tethered in the shade of a cottonwood tree next to the creek that flowed alongside Sweetwater's only street. "It is truly interesting how much little KC takes after Jesse," Ed commented. "For someone who wasn't sure she would make a good mother, she sure has a knack with your young 'uns."

"She does, doesn't she?" Pride was clearly evident in Jennifer's voice. "I don't think either of us were ready to be mothers but…"

"KC was lucky the two of you found her."

The memory of two bodies crumbled beside a burning Conestoga wagon flashed behind Jennifer's eyes. "It was the saddest day of my life."

"Not a good way for any young 'un to start life."

"I'm just glad KC was too young to know what happened. No child should see their parents die."

"That's true. Same with Charley's mother dying when he was born."

"Yes. But I felt so bad for Mr. Finnigan. He truly loved his wife. And son."

"Least he knew he couldn't raise the boy on his own."

"He sure surprised Jesse and me when he walked into the Goodrich Hotel that morning and said he wanted to give Charley to us."

Ed smiled at his own memory of the event. "He sure made Jesse's day."

"He surely did. She adores KC and Charley, and they adore her," she said, untying Blaze's reins.

"Seems to me," Ed said as he helped Jennifer into the saddle, "they adore the both of you."

Jennifer smiled down at the big man. "I can't imagine my life without Jesse or the children. I love them to death, Ed."

"Then you better quit yakkin' with me and get back out to your ranch and family. I bet they're all sittin' on the porch, waiting for you to ride into view. Tell Jesse and the young 'uns hello for me."

"You can tell them yourself tomorrow," Jennifer said as she tapped her heels against the flanks of her horse. "We need supplies, and Jesse is bringing the buckboard to town."

"Thanks for the warning," Ed called after her. "I'll make sure everything in the store is nailed down."

Jennifer laughed and waved without looking back. It wasn't unusual for her active daughter, given half a chance, to create havoc in Ed's store. It was a good thing Charley was less adventurous but given time, and his sister's guidance, her son would probably equal KC at finding trouble. As she rode down the street and past the Silver Slipper, Jennifer wondered about her children and what activities might have kept them occupied while she was in town. Tears clouded her vision as she counted another day spent away from her family.

Jesse was kneeling at the side of the washtub at one end of the back porch, something Jennifer had insisted on when they built the house after their log cabin was burned to the ground. Charley sat in the tub, splashing happily, his head covered in soapsuds as his mother washed the mud off him. "How do you get so dirty," Jesse grumbled.

"He just wike you, Mommy," KC giggled, wrapped in a towel and sitting on a chair beside the washtub. She had already been scrubbed clean and removed from the tub.

"Who says?"

"Momma."

"Seems Momma says the same thing about you, Sunshine," Jesse said, carefully pouring a pitcher of warm water over Charley's head.

KC grinned. "Yep." Charley sputtered water out of his mouth. "You s'posed keep dat closed, Cha-wie," KC advised helpfully. "Dat what Momma says."

"That's right." Jesse refilled the pitcher from the bucket beside her and held it up, waiting for her son to close his mouth and eyes. When they were shut tight, she poured the clean, warm water over her son. "That should do it, Charley. Let's get you dried off and dressed so you'll be nice and clean for Momma." She lifted the boy out of the tub and then stood him on the floor to towel him dry.

Charley looked in the direction Jennifer would come from town and Jesse smiled. "Momma will be here soon," she told her son, wishing Jennifer didn't have to be away so much. But she would never say anything to her wife because she knew how much Jennifer's position as Sweetwater's schoolteacher meant to her. She was just glad that lessons ended in the early afternoon and Jennifer was able to spend the rest of the day at the ranch.

"We wait for Momma on porch?" KC asked hopefully.

"Sure," Jesse agreed instantly. "Let's get you both dressed, and we'll sit on the porch and wait for Momma. Does that sound like a good idea?" she asked her son. Charley smiled and nodded.

"We sit dewe?" KC pointed to the opposite end of the back porch and the swing Jesse had spent most of the day assembling.

"We can't see Momma from back here," Jesse explained to her daughter. "We'll sit on the front porch. Grandma was baking some cookies earlier; maybe she'll bring you and Charley some."

"Cha-wie wikes cookies." Keeping a firm hold on the towel, KC dropped out of the chair. Her bare feet padded lightly on the wood planks as she walked over to stand next to her mother.

"And you don't?" Jesse asked teasingly.

"I wike cookies. But Cha-wie *we'wy* wikes cookies," she emphasized.

"That's because he wants to grow big and strong like you." Jesse poked KC in the tummy, causing the girl to burst into giggles. "Don't ya, Charley?" She lifted her son up as she stood and settled the boy into the crook of her arm.

"Yep," KC answered for her brother, then stretched her arms up to her mother, her towel dropping to the porch.

Jesse reached down, grabbing KC's hands and effortlessly pulling her up into her arm. With both children clean and dry, she carried them into the house.

Jennifer could hear her children's happy squeals as soon as she passed under the archway that marked the entrance to the ranch yard.

Charley was the first to spot Blaze trotting over the top of the hillock and began to gesture excitedly toward the rider.

Jesse left the children waiting impatiently on the porch while she stepped down to the ground so she could greet Jennifer first. Charley started crawling toward the edge of the porch, but his sister stopped him.

"Wait, Cha-wie," KC whispered loudly into her brother's ear. "Dey gots ta kiss."

Jesse chuckled. When Blaze stopped alongside her, she took hold of the reins, then reached up to assist Jennifer out of the saddle. When they were standing side by side, Jesse hugged Jennifer tightly before pressing their lips together. It was several heartbeats before Jesse released her wife.

"See, dey gots ta kiss fiwst," KC told Charley.

The women smiled knowingly at each other. "Missed you, darlin'." Jesse placed another tender kiss on her wife's lips.

Jennifer sighed, resting her forehead against Jesse's for a moment. "I missed you, too."

Jesse pulled the cane out of the otherwise empty rifle scabbard and handed it to Jennifer. "Go on. They've missed you, too. I'll see to Blaze. Mom's in the kitchen," she called out as she led the horse toward the barn.

Rather than climbing the steps immediately, Jennifer walked right up to the edge of the porch and opened her arms wide for the children. KC rushed into her mother's arms, kissing her several times before her brother could crawl to them. Jennifer lifted the baby up so he could wrap his arms around her neck. "Were you good today?" Jennifer asked between kisses and hugs.

"Yep," KC answered.

A little too forcefully, her mother thought. Charley's head bobbed up and down in agreement with his sister. Jennifer smiled, sure there was more to learn about the children's activities.

"Gwamma make cookies," KC reported. "Cha-wie eat two aw by hiss'f."

"Oh? And how many did you eat?" Jennifer asked.

KC held up two fingers. "Twos."

"KC?" Jennifer's tone told the child she wanted the truth.

KC frowned. "Thwee. Dey was goods," she said, as if the explanation would get her out of the trouble she had gotten herself into by not telling her mother the truth. Her lower lip quivered, poking out in the beginning of a pout.

Jennifer fought to keep the smile off her face as she set Charley back on the porch. "Let me get up there with you, and we'll go see what your grandma is up to."

KC hopped back a few steps, hoping she had avoided any punishment. "Come on, Cha-wie," she urged, tugging on the boy's britches.

Jennifer climbed the steps, then crossed to the screen door, pulling it open for KC to scamper through. She waited for Charley to reach her, then bent down and scooped the crawling baby up into her arms. "I missed you today, little man." She buried her face into his neck, blowing raspberries against his soft skin and laughing when Charley burst into loud giggles. She carried him inside and followed KC into the kitchen.

"Hi, Marie," Jennifer greeted her mother-in-law. "I hear you made some *goods* cookies today."

Marie smiled. "Hi, honey. Did she tell you she snuck one off the table?"

"No." Jennifer looked over at KC, who was trying to look innocent. "That must explain the extra one she said she ate."

"She would have snatched one or two more if Jesse hadn't come in to sneak a couple for herself and caught KC." Marie laughed. The similarities between her daughter and granddaughter grew by the day. "Jesse had a hard time trying to punish KC for doing the same thing she'd done. They ended up sharing another cookie."

Jennifer laughed. "What am I going to do with those two?" She pulled out a chair from the table and sat down, holding Charley in her lap. "Good thing my little man doesn't take after them," she murmured, nuzzling the boy's head.

"Give him time." Marie pulled out a chair and sat beside Jennifer, noticing the drawn features. "You look tired. Want me to stay around and make supper tonight?" she asked as KC climbed into her lap.

"No, I'm fine," Jennifer replied, but she wasn't very convincing.

"You sure?"

Jennifer sighed. "I'm just a little tired. I didn't sleep very well last night."

"Anything wrong?"

"No, everything's fine," Jennifer reassured her mother-in-law.

"I worry about you trying to do too much — what with raising a family, teaching school, and helping run the Slipper. And now you have the dress shop, too."

"There's no need to worry. Bette Mae pretty much runs the Slipper, and Ruthie has become quite a good businesswoman. But thank you. As for your offer, I think Jesse and I should be able to handle supper tonight."

"All right," Marie agreed reluctantly. "Then I'd best be getting back to start supper for Stanley."

KC twisted her head around to look at her grandmother. "Gwumps?"

Marie laughed at the use of the nickname only KC could get away with using. "He's been out all day and will be hungry when he gets home," she told her granddaughter.

"Oh." KC turned back around.

"What's he been up to?" Jennifer asked.

"A few of the cows wandered off to the south end of the range again," Marie explained. "With Jesse having to stay here with the children, he went off to round them up before they got themselves lost in the Badlands."

Jennifer sighed. Jesse would have done anything for her father not to have to spend the day in the saddle, anything but leave her children, especially KC who continued to refuse to be out of sight of at least one of her mothers at all times. *If only I'd been home instead of in town, Jesse would have been able to ride after the cattle instead of Stanley.*

"Ah, here you are," Jesse said, entering the kitchen from the back porch. KC scooted off her grandmother's lap, running as quickly as she could for her mommy. "Poppa is back," Jesse told her mother as she swung KC up into the air, then safely caught her in her arms.

"I better get moving then." Marie stood. "Let her do the cooking tonight," she said, patting Jennifer on the shoulder. "It'll do her good."

Jesse waited until her mother left then sat in the vacant chair beside her wife. "Something I need to know about, darlin'?"

"Your mother thinks you should cook more often," Jennifer fibbed.

Jesse smirked. "Mom hasn't eaten enough of my cookin', then." She bounced KC on her knee. "Did you tell Momma about her surprise?"

"Nope."

"What say we show it to her now?"

"Yep." With her mother's help, KC scrambled down to the floor and raced to the back door.

Jennifer watched her daughter scamper onto the back porch, then stop and wait for the others while bouncing excitedly from one foot to the other. "A surprise?"

"Yep." Jesse smiled as she offered a hand to Jennifer and pulled her to her feet. "Got ya somethin' to help you rest at the end of the day." Jesse lifted Charley out of Jennifer's arms before leading her wife to the back porch.

"Oh, my goodness!" Jennifer exclaimed when she saw the muddy water still in the washtub and the dirty clothes and towels strewn about the porch.

Jesse shrugged sheepishly. "Guess I forgot to clean up after their bath, darlin'. Leave it," she told Jennifer who was bending over to pick up the mud-encrusted shirt Charley had been wearing earlier. "I'll take care of those later. Come see your surprise."

Jennifer turned away from the tub to see her wife and daughter standing beside the swing, beaming at her.

"Oh, Jesse!" Jennifer cried, limping toward them. "When did you get this?"

"Ordered it a couple of months ago." Jesse held the swing still while her wife sat down. "Ed finally got the shipment a few days ago, and Billie brought it out this morning after you were at school. Wanted it to be a surprise." She sat beside Jennifer and waited for KC to climb aboard before she started to push with her long legs to gently move the swing. "While these two were seeing how much mud they could wear, I put it together and hung it up."

"By yourself?"

"Billie offered to help, but I knew he wanted to get back to town to Ruthie. Wasn't too much trouble."

Jennifer leaned against Jesse. After several quiet minutes, she said, "This is nice, sweetheart."

"I'm glad you like it, darlin'." Jesse wrapped an arm around her wife's shoulders. "Thought you'd like a nice place to sit and watch the sunsets."

"Only if you sit with me," Jennifer said, leaning into her wife's embrace.

"Wouldn't be anyplace else, darlin'."

CHAPTER TWO

Jesse was blowing on a spoonful of oatmeal before feeding it to Charley, who sat in the high chair in front of her. KC had pulled her own chair next to Jesse and was kneeling on the seat in order to eat scrambled eggs and bacon from her own plate. Jennifer carried a pot of coffee to the table before sitting down to the plate of eggs, bacon, and biscuits waiting for her. She placed an envelope on the table. "Ed brought this by the schoolhouse yesterday."

"Open it, Mommy!" KC cried excitedly. She enjoyed getting mail. If it was from her grandmother or one of her uncles, it usually contained a small treat for her and her brother.

"First, you finish up your breakfast," Jesse told her daughter.

KC pouted, her lower lip quivering. "Pease?"

"Nope." Jesse held back a smile at the adorable pout. "We don't want Momma to be late to school, do we?"

"Nope," KC agreed softly.

"We'll read it on the way to town, okay?"

"Okay." KC cheered right up and returned to her breakfast.

"Slow down, sweetie," Jennifer gently scolded KC, who was shoving bites of egg into her mouth as fast as she could. KC did as she was told.

"Who's it from?" Jesse asked, keeping an eye on KC to make sure she didn't start gulping food again.

Jennifer laughed. "You know, I didn't even look. I was in such a hurry to get home that I just put it in my pocket. I completely forgot about it until this morning."

Jesse flipped the envelope right side up. "It's from Granite. Who do we know in Granite?"

"No one I can think of," Jennifer replied thoughtfully as she poured coffee into two cups. "Maybe we should open it now."

KC looked up excitedly, and Jesse handed the envelope to her daughter. "Go on, Sunshine, but be careful; we want to be able to read the letter."

KC grabbed the envelope, pulling it into her lap as she sat back, adjusting her position to sit properly on her chair. She carefully tore the end of the envelope open, removing only the barest fraction of paper, then she pulled the letter out and triumphantly held it up for her mothers to see she hadn't ripped it. As soon as Jesse took the letter from her, KC turned her attention back to the envelope, peering into it to see what treats awaited. "It empty," she muttered, tossing the useless envelope on the floor.

"KC Branson," Jennifer scolded.

Knowing she was in trouble, KC slipped off her chair to retrieve the envelope. "Sowwy, Momma," she said, climbing back into her chair. "Hewe," she held the envelope out to Jennifer. "It empty," she repeated, as if that was ample reason to discard it.

"It's bad enough I have to clean up after your mommy," Jennifer pulled KC into her lap. "I don't think I should have to clean up after you, too." She tickled KC to let her know she wasn't really mad at her.

"Hey," Jesse protested, "I clean up after myself."

Jennifer grinned. "Where did I find your shirt this morning? And your britches?"

"Well, darlin'," Jesse drawled, "I was a little busy last night when I took them off." She smiled, recalling carrying her wife up the stairs to their bedroom to make love.

"I guess you were at that."

Jesse smirked, then turned her attention to the letter.

"What's it say?" Jennifer asked as she tried to rub away the blush coloring her cheeks.

"It's from Leevie."

"Leevie? I was just thinking the other day that we haven't heard from her in some time." Leevie Temple was the schoolteacher in Bannack who had befriended the women when they had visited the mining camp. "My goodness, why is she writing from Granite?"

"Only one way to find out," Jesse said as she prepared to read the letter to her family.

> *My dearest friends,*
> *I'm sorry it has taken me so long to answer your letters, but your last two have just now found their way to me. I meant to write and tell you that I was leaving Bannack, but there were so many things I had to do before I left town that it simply slipped my mind. I am living in Granite now, with someone who is very dear to my heart. There is so much to tell you that I'm not sure where to begin.*
> *I should have been more forthright when we first met. Forgive me, but I just couldn't bring myself to confide in you. For the last several years, I have loved a wonderful person and she has finally persuaded me to*

live with her. I have to say that it was seeing how happy you all are that did most of the persuading.

It is hard to admit, but things are not going as well as we had hoped. Dannie runs a freight wagon between Granite and Philipsburg, but even with all the activity in the two towns, loads have been lacking. And, I had expected to continue my teaching here, however, I was surprised to discover the town has an abundance of women qualified and willing to teach school.

Yet, we are together, and that is what truly matters.

I must close for now as Dannie will be home soon, and I promised her a walk before supper. Thank you for your wonderful letters. It's so much fun to hear how little KC and Charley are growing.

My love to all of you, Leevie.

P.S. Please come and visit sometime. Our home is small, but there is always room for such good friends as you. And I would love for Dannie to meet you. She has heard so much about you, I'm sure she would like to see that you really do exist.

Hugs to all.

"Seems you were right," Jesse told Jennifer.

"About what?"

"About Leevie. Remember?"

Jennifer smiled. She did remember. They had been saying their goodbyes to Leevie before leaving Bannack with the baby they had decided to keep and raise as their own. Leevie had smiled at them and said, *"I'd say that KC is one lucky little girl to grow up with two loving mothers. You take care of each other. You have something special, don't lose it."*

"I asked you if you thought she was like us."

Jesse nodded.

"I wonder what she's not telling us," Jennifer said as she reread the letter.

Jesse wiped cereal off Charley's chin, then held a glass of milk for the baby to take a drink. "What makes you say that?"

Jennifer frowned. "Why are they having such a rough time of it? It seems like there would be more than enough freight business to keep Dannie busy."

"Probably has to do with her being a woman. Driving a team of horses up the roads to the mining camps is rough work; there are few that can do it without losing their loads or injuring the teams. Men ain't likely to take kindly to a woman showing them up." Jesse stood. "Charley needs fresh britches before we leave."

Jennifer set her daughter on the floor. "Take KC with you and wash her face."

"Okay. Come on, Sunshine," Jesse reached a hand down for KC to grab hold of. With an easy swing of her strong arm, she lifted KC up to her chest. "Ugh," she teased the girl with egg smeared on the face. "Did you get any of that in your tummy?"

KC nodded. "Wots."

Jennifer watched Jesse carry the children out of the kitchen, then pushed herself up from the table and started to gather the dirty dishes. As she did, she considered her wife's comment.

Jesse had told her of the opposition she had faced from many of the ranchers and businessmen in Sweetwater when she had arrived and turned the Silver Slipper into a respectable business. The resentment had grown when Jesse purchased the ranch with the intention of raising cattle. It wasn't accepted that a woman could run a business in the frontier unless it was a rooming house, laundry, or eating house. Or a brothel. She wondered why men had to think so little of women. Why couldn't they understand that women were capable of endeavors other than raising children, cleaning, and cooking?

Jennifer carried the dirty dishes to the wash sink, then limped to the end of the counter where a bucket sat under the well spout. Pumping the handle, she filled the bucket and carried it to the sink. She would use the clean water to rinse the dishes after they had been scrubbed. As she slipped her hands into the warm water Jesse had filled the sink with before breakfast, she looked out the window. The sun was just beginning to peek over the mountains in the east and the morning sky was tinged in pinks and reds. Jennifer smiled. *This is home; this is where I want to be. If only I didn't have to go into town each day to teach.* A thought floated into her mind. "Maybe..." she whispered to herself.

"All nice and clean," Jesse said as she carried the children back into the kitchen. "Now, you play with your toys," she said, placing them on the floor beside their toy box. "And keep clean."

Her moccasin-covered feet moving silently across the wood floor, KC walked over and peered into the box. She dug around before pulling out a small wooden bird painted in bright colors. "Hewe, Cha-wie, you pway wit' dat." She dropped the toy in front of her brother.

Charley frowned. Crawling up to the box, the baby pulled himself upright and pushed up onto his tiptoes to look at the jumble of toys inside. Pointing, he let loose a string of baby gibberish that KC seemed to understand.

"Okay," KC said, annoyed. She pulled a stuffed dog out of the box, a gift from Jennifer's mother, and dropped it on the floor for Charley.

Charley let go of the toy box, plopping down on the floor beside the dog. Happily, he pulled the dog to his chest.

KC went back to digging through the toys, her body bent in half over the edge of the box. "Dewe you aw!" she exclaimed when she spotted what she was looking for. Standing upright, she clutched a fist-sized wooden horse in her hand. "Wook, Cha-wie." She showed the horse to her brother. "Baze."

"With all of those toys to choose from, she always seems to pull that horse out of the box," Jesse commented as her daughter's favorite toy reappeared.

"I'm surprised that horse is still in one piece," Jennifer said. The wooden horse had been KC's first toy, and she seemed to never tire of playing with it.

"I hate to think of the day something does happen to it," Jesse said, wiping the table with a damp cloth.

Jennifer rinsed the last of the dishes, then dried it off with a towel. "We're almost done in here, why don't you go get Boy hitched up?"

"Okay. But give me a few minutes." Jesse rinsed out the cloth she had been using and stretched it over the windowsill to dry. "I want to talk to Poppa, if he's around."

Jennifer leaned against Jesse. "Take your time. We'll wait on the porch."

Jesse wrapped her arms around her wife. "Bit chilly this morning, darlin'. Stay inside; I'll come in when I'm ready."

Jennifer placed her forehead against Jesse's, breathing in her scent. "I love you."

"I love you, darlin'." Jesse shifted to gently press her lips against Jennifer's.

Charley chose that moment to point at the toy box and release some more gibberish in hopes his sister would provide another toy for him to play with.

"Hush, Cha-wie," KC admonished her brother. "Mommy kissin' Momma."

Charley shook his head. "Pffttpp."

KC nodded. "Yep."

Jesse didn't have to do anything to get her big draft horse to pull to a stop at the beginning of the gravel path to the schoolhouse; Boy was so used to the trip from the ranch to town that he didn't need much guidance.

"I'll walk you up, darlin'," Jesse said, wrapping the reins around the wagon's brake handle.

Jennifer smiled. She liked it when Jesse took the time to escort her to school, then stay until the children started to arrive, giving the couple precious time together.

Jesse climbed down from the wagon, then reached back up for her wife. After helping Jennifer to the ground, she pulled the cane from under the wagon seat and handed it over. "Ready, Sunshine?" she asked, walking to the back of the wagon to release the children.

"Yep." KC was standing at the rear of the wagon bed, her arms outstretched as she waited impatiently for her mother to lift her out. "Momma, I coming," KC called out to Jennifer, who was waiting for Jesse and the children.

Once the girl was standing at her feet, Jesse ruffled KC's fine ginger-colored hair. "There ya go." Then she lifted Charley into her arms. "Come on, little man. Let's go walk your momma to school." Charley smiled, his little arm pointing at Jennifer. "That's right, Charley." Jesse kissed the boy's cheek. "That's your momma." She carried the baby to Jennifer, KC having already joined her. "Ready?"

"Yes," Jennifer said. "KC, hold my hand, sweetie. I don't want you stumbling on the gravel."

KC reached up, wrapping one hand around Jennifer's fingers and the other around Jesse's. "Okay. I weady."

The family walked across the footbridge spanning the creek and then up the gravel path to the schoolhouse.

Ed Granger watched from the porch of his store. Built by the Eastern investment company that had expected to reap huge profits out of a gold mine near Sweetwater, the two-story building had originally been designed as a hotel. When the mine turned out to be nothing more than an empty hole in the side of a hill, the investment company had pulled out of Sweetwater, selling the building to Ed as a way to recoup some of its losses. Ed took over the first floor for his mercantile, moving his inventory from the outgrown store across the street. He leased a corner of the floor to the stage line for a depot to replace the crumbling adobe building it had also outgrown. The second floor had been divided into living quarters for himself and an apartment rented by Billie Monroe and his wife, Ruthie.

"They make a fine lookin' family, don't they?" Billie said, stepping out onto the porch.

"That they do," Ed agreed without taking his eyes off Jesse and Jennifer.

"I'm glad they've got the young 'uns." Billie nudged Ed's arm.

Ed glanced down to see Billie was holding two cups of steaming coffee. "Thanks," he said, accepting one of the cups. He raised the cup to his mouth and took a sip of the hot liquid. "Speaking of young 'uns, how's Ruthie this morning?"

Billie grinned, his eyes twinkling with the pride he felt for his pregnant wife. "She's sleeping in. I told her I'd go back up in 'bout an hour to help her get dressed to go to the shop."

Ed took another sip. "Thought Jennifer told her not to worry about the shop until after the baby comes."

"She did, but you know Ruth." Billie leaned against a post that supported the porch roof. "If she doesn't have something to keep her hands busy, she goes crazy. Made her promise not to overdo it," he told the storekeeper. "And I'm sure Bette Mae will make sure she keeps that promise."

Ed laughed. "I'm sure she will."

Bette Mae managed the Silver Slipper, a brothel Jesse had won in a poker game and turned into a respectable boarding house and restaurant. It sat at the end of Sweetwater's one and only street, the only two-story building in town until the building Ed now owned had been built. Bette Mae was older than most of the women working at the Slipper and had naturally become a surrogate mother to them as well as to Jesse and Jennifer.

"You going to the Slipper for breakfast?" Billie asked, even though he knew that his friend ate at the dining room every morning.

"Yes. But I think I'll wait for Jesse to come by," Ed said as he watched the rancher walk out of the schoolhouse, her arms full of her giggling children. "I'll walk over with her."

"Afraid KC will do something in the store again?" Billie teased.

The little girl's adventures were becoming legendary in Sweetwater and had forced the storekeeper to construct what he referred to as a "holding pen" to keep KC confined anytime she visited the store.

Ed smirked. "Now that she has Charley to help her, I don't think Jesse can afford to keep covering the costs of the trouble that child manages to get herself into."

Billie chuckled. "Ain't that the truth."

"Morning, boys," Jesse greeted as she approached the mercantile. "How's Ruthie?" she asked Billie.

"Still in bed."

"Good." Jesse climbed the steps to the porch. "Jennifer's worried about her."

KC squirmed in Jesse's arm. "Mommy, down."

Jesse kept a firm grip on the girl. "Nope. We won't be here long enough for you to make any trouble." She winked at Ed. "Bette Mae's waiting for us at the Slipper, but I wanted to give you Jennifer's shopping list." She tried to reach the paper in her shirt pocket but was prevented from doing so because of the children she carried. "Sunshine, get the list out of my pocket," she told KC.

"Okay." KC pushed her hand into the pocket, her searching fingers pressing against her mother's breast.

Jesse was more than a little uncomfortable at the girl's actions. "Uh, KC...get the list. Quick."

Ed and Billie smirked, enjoying their friend's distress.

"Hewe 'tis." KC finally pulled the paper free. "Momma wants dis stuff, pease," she said, holding the list out to the storekeeper.

Ed made a show of taking the list from the girl. "Thank you, Miss KC. I will make sure that your momma gets everything she's asked for. I'll bet there's even some goodies for you and Charley on this here list," he told her.

KC grinned. "Yep, Momma puts wots a' goodies on dewe."

Ed laughed out loud at the serious reply, Billie and Jesse joining in.

"Come on, you little rascal," Jesse tickled KC's side, "let's go see Bette Mae. You coming?" she asked the men.

Ed nodded. "Sure am."

"You go on ahead," Billie told them. "I'm going to go check on Ruth."

Jesse passed on the message her wife had given her before she left the schoolhouse. "You be sure to tell her Jennifer will be coming by after school."

"I will." Billie took the empty coffee cup from Ed's beefy hand and turned to go back into the building.

"Let's go," Ed told Jesse. "I'm hungry."

"Me, too," KC chimed in.

"You're always hungry, Sunshine," Jesse grumbled. "I swear, Ed," she told the chuckling storekeeper, "if I didn't know better, I'd think she was hollow inside."

"You better hope Charley doesn't turn out the same way." Ed lifted KC out of Jesse's arms and swung her up to sit on his shoulders. Then he plucked Jesse's Stetson off her head and handed it up to KC who put it on, grinning widely. Jesse swung Charley up over her now bare head, and the children giggled all the way to the Silver Slipper.

"I was beginnin' ta think I'd not be seein' my babies today," Bette Mae complained as Jesse and Ed entered the Slipper's dining room.

"We walked Jennifer to school," Jesse explained as the older woman rushed to greet the children.

"Oh, my babies!" Bette Mae exclaimed, gathering the children into her arms. Hugging KC and Charley to her bosom, she planted kisses on their faces until both were squealing with laughter.

Ed and Jesse took seats at one of the unoccupied tables, knowing it would be several minutes before Bette Mae finished with the children. When he thought he had been ignored long enough, Ed picked up a coffee cup and started banging it on the tabletop. "I must say, Jesse," he spoke loudly to be heard over the children's shrieks and the laughter of the other diners enjoying the impromptu floor show, "the service in this here restaurant of yours surely seems to be lacking. What's a poor workin' man like myself supposed to do to get a cup of hot coffee?"

Bette Mae plopped into a chair beside Jesse. "Lordy, Ed, ya can't be begrudgin' me a little time ta say howdy ta my babies," she groused playfully.

Charley, a little overwhelmed by his sister's and Bette Mae's enthusiastic displays, reached for Jesse, who rescued the baby and sat him in her lap.

"Oh, is that what you was doing?" Ed teased back. "The way they was crying and carryin' on, I thought ya was afflicting them young 'uns somethin' awful."

"Puh." Bette Mae pursed her lips together to glare at the snickering man.

KC, now sitting in Bette Mae's lap, looked up hopefully at the woman. "Food, pease."

"Don' ya tell me yer mommy didn' feed ya this mornin'," Bette Mae sympathized.

"We ate before we left the ranch," Jesse grumbled, "so don't you be feeding her again. Jennifer will have my head if you do."

Bette Mae smiled, giving KC a gentle squeeze. "How 'bout a nice big glass of fresh milk?"

KC nodded. "Cha-wie get one, too?"

"He surely can," Bette Mae agreed. "Sally, bring two big glasses of milk for my babies." Sally normally worked as the Slipper's bartender but when business was slow in the bar, she helped out where needed.

"Make that three, Sally," Jesse added. "Oh, and you better bring Ed his breakfast before he starts to eat the table."

"You got it, boss," Sally answered. "Be right back." She disappeared through the door that led into the kitchen.

"Got a load to take to Garnet," Ed was telling Jesse as he finished off his breakfast.

Jesse was holding a sleeping Charley, and KC was playing on the floor at her feet. "I don't know, Ed," Jesse said, watching KC. "That's a three-day trip and a long time to be away. It'd be a lot easier if Jennifer wasn't teaching," she added, "then they could all come with me."

"I understand, Jesse. It's just with Billie not wanting to leave Ruthie until the baby comes, I don't have many options." Billie, once Sweetwater's sheriff, had given up his badge when he'd asked Ruthie to marry him, and now he worked for Ed in the store and driving the freight wagon. "It's hard to find anyone willing to make my deliveries, especially to the mining camps."

"Let me talk to Jennifer. I'd like to help out and we can always use the extra cash, but I hate to be away from her and the young 'uns that long."

"Fair enough." Ed popped the last bite of toast into his mouth. "I'll check with some of the cowboys in town. Maybe one of them would be interested."

KC yawned, rubbing her eyes. "Looks like I best get these two put down for their naps," Jesse said as KC tried to climb into her lap but discovered it occupied by her brother.

"Ti-wed, Mommy," KC mumbled, leaning against Jesse's leg.

Jesse shifted Charley so she could lift KC, then made sure she had a good hold on the babies before standing. "Let's see if Bette Mae will let you sleep in her room."

"Need a hand?" Ed asked, seeing the woman adjusting her hold on her children as she stood.

"Thanks, but I think I've got them. I'll let you know about Garnet when we pick up the supplies later."

"Three days?" Jennifer was not at all happy with the prospect of her wife being away that long. Jesse and the children had come to pick her up after school, and the rancher had just finished telling her of Ed's offer. "What are you going to do?"

Jesse frowned. "I don't want to do it but with Billie staying close for Ruthie, Ed's kinda in a bind. The supplies have to be delivered." She was standing by one of the windows that lined the side of the schoolhouse. From there she could see Ed working among the stacks of boxes and crates on the loading dock at the rear of the mercantile.

Jennifer walked over to stand beside Jesse. Leaning against her, she sighed, "I don't want you to go, sweetheart. I feel so alone when you're gone." Over the previous year, Jesse had made several trips for Ed, many of them as long or longer than the one they were discussing.

Jesse wrapped her arm around Jennifer's shoulders. Through the window, she watched a cowboy come out of the back of store and say something to Ed. The men talked for a few minutes, then shook hands, and the cowboy disappeared back into the store. "Maybe Ed found someone else to make the trip," Jesse said, hoping she hadn't misread the interaction between the men. She turned to look into Jennifer's eyes. "Either way, darlin', I promise this will be the last time for a while."

"Thank you," Jennifer whispered. When Jesse pressed their lips together, she leaned into the kiss.

CHAPTER THREE

Weeks had passed since Jesse had made her promise to Jennifer. The days were growing longer and warmer, and the ground had finally dried out, making it easier to attend to chores around the ranch. Jesse was mucking out the horse stalls in the barn. KC worked beside her mother, using a miniature shovel made especially for her, scooping up horse biscuits and dropping them into a bucket that Jesse would periodically empty into the wheelbarrow. Charley, playing with a few favorite toys, sat on a blanket spread out over a bed of fresh hay and surrounded by hay bales to prevent him from crawling off.

Outside, Jesse's father was repairing a section of corral that had been damaged over the winter when a tree branch blew into it. Stanley looked up from his work. "Rider coming," he called into the barn as he pulled a kerchief from his back pocket to wipe his brow.

Jesse sped to the barn door. Looking across the ranch yard, she saw a horse galloping down the hillock. The rider's flaming red hair flying behind in the wind gave away her identity. "Come on, Sunshine," she called to KC as she hurried back to the stall. She lifted KC into her arms, then did the same to Charley. "Poppa, can you saddle Dusty?" Jesse asked as she ran with the children toward the house.

Startled from her work in the garden when her daughter charged past, Marie asked, "What's wrong?"

"Sally's coming." Without breaking stride, Jesse leapt up onto the porch on her way to the kitchen and the water pump inside. Setting Charley on the floor first, she put KC down on the counter next to the basin. Pumping the handle to get water flowing, she grabbed the soap bar and began lathering her hands. "Here," she handed the soap bar to KC, "scrub as much of that stuff off your hands and face as you can. We need to go to town."

"See Momma?" KC asked as she obeyed her instructions.

Jesse smiled at her daughter. "Yep, to see your momma. And your Aunt Ruthie; she's having her baby."

"Wike Cha-wie?" KC mumbled through soap bubbles as she scrubbed her face.

"Yep." Jesse pumped the handle a few more times and rinsed her hands and face in the cold water that flowed into the basin. Picking up a towel, she dried her daughter's face and hands. As she lifted Charley to the basin, her nose wrinkled. "But we need to change Charley's britches before we go."

"You take care of him," Marie said as she bustled into the kitchen. "I'll finish up with KC."

Jesse carried Charley across the room. When she entered the sitting room and turned to take him upstairs, she saw Sally hurrying up the front steps. "We're in here," Jesse called out to the redhead.

"Miss Jennifer said to tell you to hurry," Sally panted, the screen door banging shut behind her.

"How soon?" Marie asked.

Gasping for breath, Sally managed to answer, "Bette Mae said she could deliver at any moment."

Jesse turned and ran upstairs with Charley, while Marie carried KC to the kitchen table to wait for her daughter.

Jesse wasted little time in changing her son, then rushed back downstairs. She placed the baby in his grandmother's lap and ruffled KC's hair before dashing over to the row of wood pegs near the back door where their coats were hung. She pulled the carry sack she had made when KC was a baby off one of the pegs. Slipping her arms through the straps, she quickly returned to get Charley. Sally was still standing in the doorway, breathing hard. "Get yourself a drink of water and sit for a spell," she told the redhead.

"We'll be there just as soon as Stanley gets Boy hitched to the buckboard," Marie told Jesse as she lifted Charley up to place him into the carry sack.

"You take your time, Mom." Jesse adjusted the sack to rest more comfortably on her back. "There's no reason for you to take any more of a beating on that rutted road than necessary."

"Don't you worry about us." Marie leaned over to kiss KC, now standing on a chair. "You just be careful with the babies."

"I will." Jesse held out her arms for KC. The girl jumped without fear, confident her mother would catch her. "Don't let your momma see you do that," she whispered into KC's ear. "She'll spank both of us." Jesse smiled as her daughter giggled. "There's Poppa," she said, hearing a familiar whinny. "You can ride back alongside the folks, Sally," she said as she walked out onto the back porch. Stanley was walking up beside it leading her palomino, Dusty.

"If it's all the same to you," Sally said, rubbing her sore backside, "I think I'll just stretch out in the back of the wagon."

Riding a horse was something she rarely did and never at a full gallop like today.

Jesse grinned and nodded. Walking to the edge of the porch, she swung her leg over Dusty's broad back. With KC sitting in front of her and Charley on her back, Jesse took the reins from her father. "Thanks. We'll see you in town."

Stanley nodded. "We'll be there. Now git."

A slight tap of Jesse's boots against Dusty's sides and the horse was charging toward the hillock, KC's happy squeals drifting behind.

Ed and Stanley sat on the porch of the mercantile on opposite sides of a cracker barrel with a checkerboard balanced on top. Jesse sat in a chair, tilted back against the side of the building, watching Billie nervously pace back and forth. Jesse smirked at the soon-to-be poppa. "Ya know, Billie, wearing a rut in these planks ain't gonna make that baby come any sooner." Her eyes drifted down to KC and Charley asleep on a blanket in the shade of the porch. "Besides, all that stompin' is making it hard for my babies to sleep."

Billie reached the end of the porch, turned around, and stomped back to drop into the chair beside his friend. "Damn it, Jesse, this ain't easy. First, Bette Mae says the baby could come any time," he ran his fingers through his hair, scratching his scalp, "then she says it could be a while."

Jesse took pity on the expectant father, who was more of a brother to her than a friend. She reached over and squeezed his arm. "Babies come when they're good and ready. You can't hurry them up or slow them down."

Billie sighed. "You had it easy. Yours came already hatched."

When Ed barked out a laugh, Stanley looked up from studying his available moves on the checkerboard.

Jesse chuckled. "I don't think I would have put it exactly like that, and I don't think I'd let Jennifer hear you say that, but you're right. I didn't have to go through this. That's not to say I agree with the 'having it easy' part. Before they come out is the easy part; after that, they keep you mighty busy."

"You ever regret having 'em?" Billie asked, looking at the sleeping duo. He adored Jesse's children, but he doubted he could be the parent his friend was proving to be.

"Not once," Jesse said truthfully. "Fact is, I can't imagine not having the little rascals around."

"You're happy, ain't ya, Jesse?" Billie gazed at the woman he remembered as riding into Sweetwater lonely and without a future. Now she was a successful businesswoman and married with a growing family. And her eyes had been free of sadness ever since a certain ginger-haired schoolteacher had arrived in Sweetwater. At least, until recently.

"I'm very happy, Billie."

Jesse smiled, but her eyes reflected the melancholy he had been noticing. "But?"

Jesse leaned back in the chair. "I miss Jennifer," she sighed.

"What do you mean?"

"With her teaching duties keeping her in town during the day and the ranch keeping me busy, sometimes it seems like we're just riders passing on the road. I wish she could be home more."

"You could ask her to quit," Billie suggested.

Jesse shook her head. "No. Teaching is what she wants to do; it's why she came to Sweetwater. I can't ask her to give it up anymore than she'd ask me to give up the ranch."

"But you would, wouldn't you? Give up the ranch...if she asked."

"Yes. If she asked, I would."

"Don't you think she feels the same about her teaching?"

Jesse stared at the schoolhouse sitting on a knoll not far from the mercantile. *Is Billie right? Would Jennifer be willing to give up teaching and stay home?* A newborn's cry interrupted her thoughts. Jesse jumped up, then pulled Billie to his feet. She wrapped her arms around her friend, hugging him tight. "You best be gettin' up there. Sounds like you're finally a poppa."

The new father stood frozen in place, and Ed slapped Billie on the back. "She's right, boy." He laughed at the mixture of fear and excitement on the young man's face. "Go on, now. Ruthie will be waiting for you." He shoved Billie toward the doorway.

Billie stumbled across the porch and through the open door. By the time he reached the stairs leading up to the living quarters, his brain had finally caught up to the situation. Taking the steps three at a time, he raced up to meet his first child. Jennifer was coming down the stairs and had to flatten herself against the wall to avoid being bowled over. "I'm a father." Grinning, he pulled Jennifer into a hug, kissing her on the cheek. "I'm a father," he repeated as he released her and continued upstairs.

Jennifer laughed as she watched the animated man disappear down the hallway.

Jesse climbed the steps to meet Jennifer. "That birthin' took quite a long while for you to be standing. You okay, darlin'?"

"I'm fine." Jennifer looked at her wife. "It's a boy, a fine healthy boy," she said as Jesse wrapped her arms around her.

"He'll like that," Jesse murmured, kissing Jennifer's forehead. "How's Ruthie?"

"Fine. Tired, but fine. Bette Mae said the baby didn't tear her much."

"Good."

"Speaking of babies," Jennifer leaned into Jesse, "where are ours?"

"Sleeping." Jesse gave Jennifer an arm to lean on as they moved carefully down the stairs. "Poppa and Ed are keeping an eye on them."

As she stepped out on the porch, Jennifer called to her father-in-law and the storekeeper, "Thanks for watching them."

"They don't make much trouble when they're sleeping. Too bad you can't keep 'em that way," Ed grumbled, but his eyes were twinkling as he teased the mothers.

"Well, what was it?" Stanley asked, placing his elbow on the checkerboard and dislodging most of the playing pieces.

"A baby boy," Jesse said proudly, even though she'd had nothing to do it.

"Well, I'll be." Ed beamed. "Bet Billie is bustin' off his buttons at that news. And Ruthie?"

"She's fine," Jennifer answered, sitting in the chair Jesse placed behind her. "Bette Mae and Marie are cleaning her up." She turned to look up at Jesse, an apologetic look on her face. "I couldn't stand any longer."

"Hush." Jesse gently cupped her hands around Jennifer's cheeks, smoothing out the worry lines in her forehead. "You did what you could, darlin'. Ruthie wouldn't ask for any more."

Jennifer leaned into the caress, closing her eyes as she let her wife's love soak into her.

"You look tired, daughter," Stanley told Jennifer. "You should take her over to the Slipper so she can get some rest, Jesse."

"No, I'm all right," Jennifer protested, trying to hold back a yawn.

"Poppa is right, darlin'." Jesse grinned when Jennifer gave in willingly. "Let me gather up the young 'uns and we'll walk over. Or do you want me to get the buckboard?" The wagon was in front of the Silver Slipper where Stanley had left it when he and Marie arrived in town.

"No, I can walk," Jennifer said. "It might help to stretch out the leg after standing for so long."

Jesse knelt down and carefully lifted the sleeping babies into her arms. With the children secured, she returned to Jennifer, who was already standing, leaning heavily on her cane. "Ready, darlin'?"

"Yes. Will you tell Billie and Ruthie we'll come back later?" Jennifer said to Ed and Stanley.

Stanley smiled at his daughter-in-law. "You go on now, it'll be a while before Ruthie is ready for company. Marie slept for a week after givin' birth to that wife of yours. But I'm thinkin' she was just resting up for the trouble to come. I never heard a baby holler as much as Jesse did in those first weeks."

"Come on, darlin'." Jesse waited until Jennifer wrapped a hand around her arm. "Let's go before he thinks of any other lies to tell about me." She grinned at her father and he grunted.

When Jennifer woke she was alone in bed, but the whispered voices of her wife and daughter told her they were somewhere in the room. She rolled onto her side in the direction of the voices.

"Mommy," KC whispered, "we see baby?"

"Yep, Sunshine," Jesse whispered back. She was kneeling on the floor, bent over Charley, changing his britches. KC was sitting beside her. "Just as soon as your momma wakes up."

"Mommy?" KC whispered again. "Do baby stink wike Cha-wie?"

Jesse chuckled, poking KC in the ribs which caused the girl to burst into quiet giggles. "Yep. Just like Charley. And just like you do when you need a bath."

"I don' need baff," KC protested, scooting away from Jesse's probing finger.

"Oh yes, you do, and so do I." Jesse sniffed loudly. "Remember what we were doing before we came to town this morning?"

"And what were you two smelly things doing?" Jennifer asked.

"Momma!" KC and Charley cried at the same time.

KC hopped up and ran for the bed, scrambling up onto the chest at the foot of the bed to reach her mother. "Momma," she wrapped her arms around Jennifer's neck, "we go see baby now."

Jennifer rolled onto her back, her arms wrapped around KC. "*It* is a baby boy," she said, tweaking the girl's nose. "And I refuse to go anyplace with you until you have a bath. Just what were you doing this morning, Jesse?"

"Mucking out the barn." Jesse sat on the bed with Charley. The baby pushed out of her lap to crawl to Jennifer, and Jesse bent down to give her wife a kiss. "Sorry, we didn't have much time to wash up after Sally rode in with the news. I'll see if the bathing room is available since it looks like we'll be spending the night in town. I hope the folks thought to bring a change of clothes for all of us."

"Knowing your mother, I'm sure she did and more." Jennifer turned to look out the window. Night had fallen. "How long did I sleep?"

"A few hours." Jesse smiled. "Guess Poppa was right when he said you looked tired. Having babies must be hard work."

"It sure looked to be." Ruthie had seemed to be in a lot of pain during the birth of her son. She wondered if anything could be worth that much suffering. Charley snuggled against her, providing the answer to her question.

"You want to eat first?" Jesse asked.

"No, you need a bath, and so does KC." Jennifer laughed when Jesse made a face at her. "You might as well take Charley in with you."

"What about you?" Jesse wiggled her eyebrows. "You want to join us?"

Jennifer smirked. "As much as that offer intrigues me, it really isn't that appealing to bathe with you as you wash horse biscuits and who knows what else off."

"You don't know what you're missing, does she, Sunshine?"

"Nope." KC grinned, wiggling about to give her momma a good whiff of her.

"Arrrgh!" Jennifer cried. "Jesse, get her off of the bed before we have to wash the blankets, too."

"Come on, you rascal." Jesse stood and lifted KC up by her britches. "Leave your momma alone before she makes me sleep on the floor tonight."

"I seep wit' you, Mommy," KC said, hanging in mid-air.

"Ain't the same, Sunshine." Jesse carried the baby out the door. "It just ain't the same."

"Hmmm." Jennifer tickled Charley. "Seems your mommy forgot something."

Jesse reappeared. "Sorry." She picked the baby up by his britches. Holding both children out at arm's length, she bent down to kiss Jennifer.

Jennifer smiled. "I love you, Jesse Branson."

"We'll be in the bathing room if you need us." She spun around and carried the giggling babies out of the room.

Jesse was sitting cross-legged on the floor in Billie and Ruthie's sitting room, KC draped over her shoulder watching the infant sleep. "What do you plan on naming him?" She nodded at the baby she held in her arms.

The room was overflowing with people. Bette Mae, Ed, Stanley, Marie, Jesse, Jennifer, KC, Charley, and the new baby and his parents were all squeezed into a room intended to hold many fewer people.

"Michael," Billie answered.

"Michael Monroe," Jesse said. "Has a nice sound to it."

"Lordy." Bette Mae couldn't help but bend over and pinch the newborn's toes. "He is jus' adorable. Ya'd never know Billie was capable of havin' such a thing."

"No, I'd say young Michael must get his looks from his momma," Jesse teased.

Charley was sitting in Jennifer's lap and turned his head up to look at his mother. Jennifer bent down and kissed her son's outstretched hand. "I'm your momma," she explained, "and Ruthie is Michael's momma." Charley twisted around in Jennifer's lap, snuggling against her breast.

Bette Mae chuckled. "I don' believes 'e quite knows wha' ya is tryin' ta tell 'im."

Jennifer cradled her tired boy in her arms. "No, I don't think he does."

"It's been a long day," Marie said. Being the only other woman in the room who had given birth to a child, she knew how tired Ruthie must be feeling. "I think it's time we left these folks alone with their baby."

"She's right, Jesse. It's time our babies went to bed, too."

Jesse carefully handed Michael to Billie, who gathered up his son, then she stood and stretched out the kinks in her long legs. "Don't you be worrying about the dress shop," she said to Ruthie. "We'll do what we can, and what we can't, can wait until you feel up to coming back."

Bette Mae laughed. "Tha's a mouthful, even for you."

"What Jesse is trying to say," Jennifer said with a grin, "is you take all the time you need."

"Thank you." Billie gingerly laid the baby in his wife's arms and Ruthie held him close. "It won't be long, I promise. I don't want anyone upset that I haven't got their dresses made."

"He's a beautiful baby." Jennifer smiled at their young friend. "You spend some time with him. I'm sure the ladies will understand why their dresses aren't finished. Besides, you don't want to miss out on this time with Michael."

Jesse could hear the regret in her wife's voice. Maybe it was time to talk to Jennifer about giving up teaching and staying at the ranch with the children. "Come on, KC." Jesse pulled the girl into her arms. "Let's take your momma and grandparents back to the Slipper."

KC swiped her arm in a wide, beckoning arc. "Come on, Gwumps. Wet's go."

Stanley began to growl while the others snickered. Jesse groaned as she stepped in front of the chair and helped Jennifer stand. "We really need to get her to stop calling him that," she whispered.

"I've tried," Jennifer whispered back.

Marie was saying her goodbyes to Billie and Ruthie and turned to address Jesse and Jennifer. "Don't worry," she whispered loud enough for everyone to hear, "he likes it, even if he does growl at her."

"Woman," Stanley huffed, "are you ready to leave or not?"

Marie winked at her daughters. "Yes, dear, I'm ready. Now come get your granddaughter so Jesse can help Jennifer down the stairs." Stanley frowned but didn't complain when KC was passed to him.

KC settled into her grandfather's arms. "Gwumps, we go Swippe' and get tweats. Okay?"

Jesse just shook her head as her father carried KC out of the room to the laughter her comment caused.

Ed chuckled, slapping Jesse on the back. "Yep, you've got your work cut out with that young 'un. You surely do."

"We'd better go, sweetheart," Jennifer slipped her arm around Jesse's, "before she talks him into something else."

"Oh, boy," Jesse groaned, taking the sleepy Charley from Jennifer. "Oh, boy."

CHAPTER FOUR

The next morning after sleeping in, Jesse walked Jennifer to the schoolhouse. It was later than Jennifer normally liked to be at school and the children were already arriving. Jesse decided to share what had been on her mind since her conversation with Billie the day before. "Darlin'—"

"Morning, Mrs. Branson." A trio of girls ran past the couple on their way to the schoolhouse.

"Yes, sweetheart?" Jennifer prompted after the children had run by.

"Morning, Mrs. Branson," a boy shouted as he hurried to the school.

"I was thinking," Jesse continued.

"Morning, Mrs. Branson. Did you get to see the baby?" another girl asked. It didn't take long for news to spread in the small town, and most had already heard that Ruthie had given birth the day before.

"Yes, I did, Kathleen," Jennifer told the girl. "What were you thinking?" she asked Jesse.

A group of boys shouted as they splashed through the creek instead of using the footbridge, "Morning, Mrs. Branson."

Jesse gave up with a shrug. "We'll talk later."

"Sweetheart?" Jennifer knew Jesse had slept little the night before, and she was worried about what could be causing her wife such distress. "Let me get them settled and busy with their lessons, then we can talk."

"No." Jesse smiled, shaking her head. "You go on. It'll keep."

"Are you sure?"

"Yep." Jesse leaned forward. Pressing her lips to Jennifer's, she ignored the giggles coming from the children waiting in front of the schoolhouse. "I love you, darlin'."

"We'll talk tonight?"

"I promise. Go on, the children are waiting."

"I love you, Jesse."

"Love you, too."

Jesse waited until Jennifer led the students into the schoolhouse before she turned to go back to the Slipper where her own children still slept under Bette Mae's watchful eyes. She and Jennifer had seen no reason to wake them since Jesse was staying in town to take care of some repairs that Bette Mae had requested at the boarding house.

"What next?" Jesse asked, pounding the final nail into a plank she had used to patch a hole in the wall. The winter winds had taken a toll on the Slipper's east side, it having taken the brunt of the harshest weather.

"Some a' them back steps from the kitch'n upstairs seem ta be a mite wobbly," Bette Mae told her boss. "I'm fearful someone's gonna take a fall on 'em."

"Okay, let's take a look." Jesse tossed her hammer into the toolbox. "Let me get Charley." Jesse had been moving the children as she went from one repair job to the next. When she was trying to work, it wasn't too convenient to have to look after the children, but the few times they had tried having KC stay at the school with Jennifer had turned into disasters. The inquisitive girl's endless questions made it impossible for Jennifer to concentrate on her students. And sending the children back to the ranch with their grandparents was not an option, considering KC's fear of having her mothers out of her sight. "Come on, KC," Jesse said. "We need to go inside now."

"Okay." KC gathered up the toys she and Charley had been playing with, then padded around the wrap-around porch to the front door. "Mommy, doah too heavy," she groaned, pushing against the wooden door with all her might.

Bette Mae chuckled at the struggling child. "Hold on, little angel. Let me help ya." She reached over KC's head, turning the knob and pushing the door open. "There ya go."

"T'anks," KC said, marching into the Slipper's dining area.

"Into the kitchen, KC," Jesse directed as she carried Charley and her toolbox inside. "We'll find a place for you and Charley to play while I take a look at the steps."

"Okay. Come on, Cha-wie," KC called to her brother, even though he was being held by Jesse. She led the group through the dining room and into the kitchen.

Jesse looked around the crowded kitchen for a safe place to put the children.

"What's wrong?" Bette Mae asked when Jesse stood frowning.

"Seems like an awful lot of places in here for the young 'uns to get into trouble. Best you stay at the foot of the stairs," she told KC.

"And what happens to them if'n ya was to fall off one of them wobbly steps?" Bette Mae asked. "I'll stretch out the blanket over here," she said, carrying the blanket to the doorway between the kitchen and the saloon. "We'll jus' prop the door open so's KC can see ya."

"But then I won't be able to see them."

"I'll keep an eye on them whilst I start the stew fer tonight."

"Is that okay, KC?" Jesse asked as her daughter sat on the blanket. "I'm going to be right there." She pointed at the steps that led upstairs from the kitchen.

KC leaned forward on her hands, craning her neck to make sure she could see up the narrow stairway. "Yep."

"Good." Jesse smiled. "You keep an eye on your brother. Don't let him wander away." She placed Charley down beside his sister.

"Okay." KC turned her attention to her brother. "Cha-wie, you stay wight hewe."

"All right, show me which steps you're complaining about." Jesse set the toolbox down at the foot of the stairs, then pulled out her hammer and a fistful of nails.

"Lordy," Bette Mae fussed, "seems ya could tell that yerself if'n ya jus' took the time ta walk up 'em."

Jesse laughed. "Maybe. But I'd rather you show me the ones bothering you so I don't get blamed for missing any."

"Don' know how's ya 'xpect a woman ta git any work done around here if'ns I have ta be showin' ya every little thing."

KC watched Jesse work her way up the steps, testing each one as she went. Satisfied that her mother wasn't leaving her, she decided to play with Charley, but when she turned toward the baby, he was no longer on the blanket. "Cha-wie," she called. He did not answer.

"Cha-wie Bwanson, wheah awe you?" she called again, trying to sound as much like her momma as possible. She heard a string of Charley's gibberish coming from inside the saloon. Pushing herself onto her feet, she went to look for her brother. "Cha-wie, come hewe. Mommy be mad."

Upstairs, in one of the Slipper's rooms, an overnight guest was waking. He'd had way too much to drink the night before and, even though it was past midday, his mind was still too groggy to make much sense of where he was or what he was doing. Having awakened with a desperate need to relieve his bladder, he dropped his arm over the edge of the bed and groped for the chamber pot.

"Damn," he muttered as he searched. "I know there has to be one here. Guess I'm just gonna have to go out back to the outhouse." He grumbled at the necessary but unwelcome prospect.

Heavy curtains covered the window, leaving the room in complete darkness. He didn't remember pulling the drapes shut the night before and decided it must still be nighttime. He reached for the candle and matches on the table beside the bed. His numb fingers fumbled with a match and it took him several tries to get it to light so he could hold it to the candlewick until a small flame flickered to life. Struggling to his feet, he flicked the spent match aside. With candle in hand, he staggered to the door.

Bright daylight flooded the room as he pulled the door open. Startled, he threw his hands up in front of his eye to block out the blinding light. The candle flew out of his hands, bouncing on the floor and rolling under the bed where a wisp of black smoke curled off the wick, its flame now extinguished.

Stumbling out into the hallway, his eyes closed tight against the harsh light, the man felt his way down the corridor to the back steps. Half falling, half walking, he lurched downward, brushing past Jesse and Bette Mae, then charging out the back door of the kitchen to the outhouse.

"Rough night?" Jesse asked Bette Mae.

"Drank more than he should have," Bette Mae said as the back door slammed against its frame and then swung wildly on its hinges. "Had ta get Ed ta help get 'im up ta his room."

"Oh." Jesse turned back to work on the steps.

Upstairs in the man's room, the match smoldered on the bed quilt as a gust of wind rushed into the room from the hallway. Moments later, the bed was engulfed in flame.

"Is that smoke?" Stopping her work on a loose step, Jesse sniffed the air. "You burnin' something?" she teased Bette Mae.

"Ya know better'n that," Bette Mae huffed, swatting Jesse on the leg.

"Do you smell that?" Jesse asked again when she detected a stronger whiff of smoke.

"Now, tha' ya mention it," Bette Mae sniffed the air, "I do smells somethin'."

Jesse took a few steps upward until she could see down the hall. Smoke was billowing out of the room at the far end. "Fire!" she called down to Bette Mae. "Get everybody outside. Hurry!" Betty Mae rushing down in front of her, Jesse was already halfway down the staircase when she finished yelling her instructions.

"I'll get the girls," Bette Mae called out, hurrying out into the dining room where Sally and a couple of the other women that worked at the Slipper were clearing tables after the midday meal.

"KC," Jesse called out, running across the kitchen to where she had left her children. Her heart stopped when she found the blanket empty. "KC, where are you!" she screamed.

Jennifer stepped out onto the schoolhouse porch to call the children back inside after the midday break.

"Mrs. Branson," one of the children called out, pointing down to the end of town. "Look...the Slipper is on fire."

Jennifer's heart stopped. Without wasting a moment, she stepped off the porch and, using her cane to support her bad leg, rushed down the gravel path. The children ran behind her, over the footbridge and down the dirt street toward the burning building. Thick black smoke was pouring out of a window at the end of the second floor, and as she watched a tongue of bright red flame burst from the window.

"Jesse!" Jennifer screamed as she ran. "Jesse, the babies! Where are the babies?"

Helping a customer inside his store, Ed heard the screams and ran outside. Seeing the smoke and flames, he charged off the down the street. "Ring the bell!" he yelled to Billie, who was a few steps behind him. Billie ran for the schoolhouse. The school bell also served as the emergency bell for the small town. By the time Billie reached the pole and started yanking on the rope to sound the alarm, the street was full of people rushing toward the Slipper.

Fire was a serious affair in a town where almost all buildings were constructed of wood. If the flames weren't contained, the entire town could be consumed, destroying people's homes and livelihoods. No effort was spared to stop every fire that got started.

Ed quickly overtook Jennifer. He scooped her up with one of his strong arms and kept running.

"Jesse!" Jennifer cried as Ed carried her to the Slipper. "Where's Jesse? Where are the babies?"

"We'll find them," Ed assured the distraught woman. "Don't you worry, we'll find them."

"Buckets," someone yelled. "We need more buckets!"

Men, women, and even the schoolchildren were using anything they could to fill with water from the horse troughs and creek. Since the fire was burning on the second floor, it was hard to throw the water high enough to have any effect on the flames.

"Get the rest of the building wet," Ed yelled when he saw men heaving water up as high as they could, only to have it fall short of the flames. "You stay put," he ordered Jennifer, setting her on her feet near the front of the building. "Billie, get that buckboard over by the side there. We can stand in it to get the water higher. Set up a bucket line," he told an older boy running past with an empty bucket. "It'll save time."

Jennifer wanted to run inside the Slipper to find her family, but she knew that would be foolish; she had no idea where in the large building they might be. All she could do was stand and wait for Jesse to come out with the children. And hope. And pray. "Jesse, please sweetheart, bring yourself and our babies out safely!" she cried.

The room on fire was located above the saloon. It didn't take long for the flames to start burning through the floor, sending acrid smoke downward into that room.

KC sniffed, rubbing her nose at the foul-smelling smoke. "Cha-wie," she called. Not seeing her brother in the main room, she walked around the end of the bar and peeked down the space between it and the wall lined with shelves of bottles and glasses. It was an area that had always intrigued her, the shiny glass drawing her attention whenever she was in the room. But her mothers had forbidden her to play around the bar, afraid she could get hurt if any of the bottles fell from their shelves. She knew she wasn't supposed to be there, but she had to find Charley.

Charley was sitting behind the bar. Hearing his sister's calls, he wriggled under a low hanging shelf, thinking it was a game to hide from KC. He giggled, listening as she looked around the room searching for him. His nose started twitching at a really bad smell. He rubbed it, trying to stop the burning sensation. He wiped his eyes, blinking to ease the irritation caused by the smoke. This time, when he heard his sister call out for him, he whimpered, hoping she'd come and take him back into the kitchen. His game wasn't fun anymore.

"Cha-wie," KC called out again, coughing a bit as the smoke around her thickened. She heard a soft whimper from the other end of the bar and headed for it. "Cha-wie, is dat you?" KC stood next to her brother's hiding place, bent over, and looked under the shelf. "Why you hiding? Come on, Mommy be mad." She reached for her brother. A fit of coughing caused her to sit abruptly, her arms waving around her head, trying to chase the smoke away.

Charley crawled out from his hiding place and into his sister's lap, sniffling and wiping at his burning eyes.

"It okay, Cha-wie." KC hugged her brother. "Don' cwy. Mommy come git us."

"Mommy," the baby whimpered.

"Yep." KC nodded in the thickening smoke. "Mommy come. You see."

"KC," Jesse yelled into the saloon, the room filling with blinding smoke. "Sunshine, where are you?"

KC sucked in a lungful of air to answer her mother, but the smoke burned her throat and all she could do was cough. "Hewe, Mommy. We hewe," she managed to rasp out.

Jesse heard the faint cry but couldn't tell where it had come from. "KC, where are you?"

As soon as he heard Jesse's voice, Charley began to cry, his sobs intermixed with coughing.

"See," KC said, rocking her brother. "Mommy comin'."

"KC!" Jesse yelled. She pushed her way into the smoke in search of her children, banging her knee hard as she walked into a table used by the saloon's patrons for their card games.

"Hewe, Mommy," KC cried out, her voice weak but unwavering.

Jesse's outstretched hands found the edge of the bar, and she followed it. "KC," she continued to call as she inched around to the end of the bar, the thick smoke preventing her from seeing more than a few inches.

"Hewe, Mommy." KC reached out and tugged on Jesse's pant leg when she saw it appear out of the smoke.

Jesse knelt down. "Is Charley with you?"

"Yep." KC's vigorous nodding was unseen by her mother. "He wight hewe. He cwyin' cuz he sca-wed."

More by feel than sight, Jesse gathered her children into her arms. "You hurt?"

"No." KC snuggled against her mother, glad to be safe in her arms.

"Okay, let's get you out of here." Jesse stood. She squinted, her eyes straining to see through the smoke. Going back to the kitchen was out of the question; the wall at that end of the room was on fire. She thought about trying to make it across the room to the door that would take them into the dining room, but without knowing how far the fire had spread, that might put them in a worse situation. "Guess the only way out is through the window." The children clung to her. "I need to sit you down for a minute," she said as she leaned forward to place the babies on top of the bar.

"Mommy," Charley cried out as Jesse set him down.

"I'm right here, little man." Jesse kissed the top of the boy's head. "Just let me get my coat fixed." She unbuttoned the jacket she'd worn that day because a chilly wind had been blowing in from the east. She tucked the bottom of the coat into her pants, forming a pocket to carry the babies in. "Okay, come on." She gathered the children back into her arms, wrapping the coat around them and fastening the buttons to keep it in place.

The smoke was getting thicker, and the end wall was being consumed by the flames. Jesse made her way to the front of the room and the row of windows that faced town. She hadn't gone more than a few feet when part of the ceiling gave way, crashing down on the other end of the bar. "Hang on, we're getting out of here!" Jesse yelled to the twosome bundled in her coat.

In her mind's eye, Jesse calculated where she needed to jump to break through a window and where she would land on the porch on the other side. From there it would be a simple jump over the railing to the safety of the ground. Hoping she remembered the location of the tables positioned about the saloon, Jesse started to run.

Charging forward, Jesse spotted a soft glow of sunlight outlining the windows; she headed for the closest one. Leaping into the air, she crashed through the glass using her shoulder as a battering ram. Her boots hit the surface of the porch, wet from the efforts of the townsfolk trying to stop the flames. Unable to control herself on the slick wood, she skidded toward the railing, her hip slamming into it. Her momentum carried her body head over tea kettle.

Jennifer saw glass explode from the window, followed by her wife's appearance. She watched in relief as Jesse landed on the porch then in horror as the catapulting body continued across the porch and cartwheeled over the railing. Jesse landed on her back with a *THUD*, the force of the landing knocking all the air out of her lungs.

"Jesse!" Jennifer screamed as she hurried to her wife's side. Dropping to her knees, she stared at her unmoving spouse. Afraid to touch her, in case she was injured, but needing to know if she was alive, she reached out and tentatively caressed the pale cheek. "Jesse, sweetheart," she whispered, "are you okay? Sweetheart, say something. Please," she pleaded.

"Ugh," was all Jesse could force out.

Tears formed in Jennifer's eyes. At least Jesse was alive. "The babies, Jesse. Where are the babies?"

KC wiggled up just enough for her head to pop out of the coat that protected her. "Hewe, Momma," KC grinned. "Cha-wie hewe too."

Jennifer was shocked to see the girl's head suddenly appear. "KC? Are you okay?"

"Yep." KC wriggled free of the coat.

Jennifer scrabbled to get the buttons undone. Once she had, she fell on top of Jesse and the exposed babies, hugging and kissing them as tears rolled down her cheeks. "You're okay," she murmured between sobs. "Thank goodness, you're okay."

"Get off me," Jesse managed to gasp. Her wife's smothering hugs were making it impossible for her lungs to fill with much needed air.

Charley wrapped his arms around Jennifer's neck, refusing to let go as she sat up. "Sweetheart, are you all right?"

"Can't breathe," Jesse wheezed.

KC was straddling the prone body, bouncing on Jesse's stomach. "Mommy, dat fun. We go ag'in?"

Jesse struggled for air, her breathing not helped by her daughter's activity. She slowly raised an arm and placed a shaky hand on top of KC's head. "Don't...bounce," she gasped.

"Okay." KC stopped bouncing and grinned hopefully. "We go ag'in?"

The sun was setting in the west, the brilliant colors of the sunset muted by the smoke that still hung in the air over Sweetwater. One end of the Silver Slipper continued to smolder, but the flames had finally been extinguished. Most folks had gone back to their own homes and businesses, thankful the fire had been contained to a single building. Bette Mae and Sally were inside the Slipper, taking inventory of the damage to the saloon and the rooms above it. Ed and Billie, with the help of some of the older schoolboys, were passing scorched furniture out of broken windows and tossing it over the porch railing into the street to prevent it from starting any new fires. Jesse sat on the steps of the Slipper, her arms wrapped around Jennifer and the children.

"What is it with us and fires?" Jennifer asked, referring to the log home she had first shared with Jesse that had also been destroyed by flames.

"Don't think we have anything to do with it, darlin'," Jesse tightened her arms around her wife. "We build everything out of wood. A fire gets started, it's hard to stop. Only thing in town safe from fire is the bank." She looked down the street at the brick and stone building, another reminder of the investment company's activity in town. "Just a fact of life out here. We're lucky folks saved as much of the Slipper as they did."

"Do you know what started it?"

"Nope." Jesse shrugged. "Probably never will."

"Well, I'm just glad you and the babies are safe."

"Me, too."

"Jesse?"

"Hmm."

"We're going to go see Leevie," Jennifer announced, the fire cementing a decision she had come to several days earlier. It had been terrifying to see the Slipper on fire and realize her family was inside. But it was the knowledge they wouldn't have been there if she hadn't needed to be at the schoolhouse that really frightened her. It was definitely time to make some changes in her life. But before she could, she had to talk to her friend.

"Right now?" Jesse asked, not surprised by her wife's comment but confused as to its timing.

"Not right now, silly." Jennifer grinned. "But as soon as the school term is completed at the end of the month, we're going to Granite."

"Okay."

"You're not going to argue?"

"Nope."

"You don't want to know why?"

"Nope." Jesse didn't really care why Jennifer was adamant about traveling to the mining camp. Right here, right now, all she cared about was that their children were safe and she had everything important to her wrapped in her arms.

"What now?" Jennifer asked, glancing over her shoulder at the ruined building.

"Let's go home."

"What about the Slipper?"

"It's not going anywhere. We'll worry about it later. Right now, I want to go home, put the babies to bed, and make love to my wife."

Jennifer sighed, melting into Jesse's embrace. "Sounds wonderful."

CHAPTER FIVE

The sound of hammers thumping against wood floated into the schoolroom where Jennifer sat at her desk reviewing the day's lessons. She knew the activity was taking place at the end of town where Jesse was working on repairing the damage to the Silver Slipper. She also knew that Ed and Billie were helping her wife; her children were there, too. She sighed. It was where she wanted to be.

The end of the school term was nearly upon her, and Jennifer was looking forward to it like she never had before. She missed being with her family during the day. She missed the moments Jesse would surprise her with a handful of freshly picked wildflowers or ride into the ranch yard to give her a kiss before galloping back out to whatever chore she had left undone. She missed watching KC and Charley play and hearing their giggles of delight when Jesse joined them.

When she first arrived in Sweetwater, she had been certain that being a schoolteacher would be wonderful. And it was. Seeing the smile on a child's face after reading aloud for the first time or adding a column of numbers and coming up with the right answer was worth all her efforts in the classroom. Children enjoyed coming to school; they liked Jennifer and she liked them. But they weren't KC and Charley, and those were the children she wanted to spend her days with.

Jennifer heard boots crunching on the gravel walk outside and smiled as she heard KC calling for her, even before her wife and daughter appeared in the schoolhouse doorway.

"Ah, here you are, darlin'," Jesse said as she entered. "Thought you'd be coming to the Slipper when school ended." She carried Charley toward the front of the schoolroom. KC was tugging at her hand to be set free, and Jesse obliged when she saw Jennifer appeared to be alone in the room.

"Momma," KC cried excitedly. She ran to Jennifer, who was still seated behind her desk. "Momma, I bang naiwes. It hawd." She pulled herself up into Jennifer's lap. "Cha-wie too smaw. He can't bang naiwes, he get huwt."

Jennifer looked at Jesse in alarm, thinking their daughter was describing an actual event. "You let Charley hammer nails?"

"He's fine, darlin'." Jesse bent over to kiss her wife and then sat on the edge of the desk. "I told her *not* to let him hammer because I didn't *want* him to get hurt."

Jennifer smiled in relief, opening her arms to the baby who was reaching for her. "Come here, little man."

Jesse handed the baby to Jennifer. "What's keepin' ya so long, darlin'? It's been almost two hours since the school bell rang. We were startin' to get worried."

"I had some papers to finish grading and Miles Jr. wanted to get some books," Jennifer explained.

A boy suddenly rose from where he had been sitting on the floor next to the bookshelves that lined one wall of the room. "Sorry, Mrs. Branson. Guess I got lost in this story and didn't know so much time had passed."

"It's all right, Miles," Jennifer assured him. "I just now finished up with these papers. Did you find something you hadn't read already?"

"No, ma'am, but I found a couple I haven't read in a while." Miles Jr., the son of Sweetwater's mayor, had been the first student for whom Jennifer had made a difference. A shy, withdrawn boy, in Jennifer's classroom he had discovered a love of reading and had read every book Sweetwater had to offer.

"Well, then, maybe you'll want to stop by the Slipper on your way home, Miles," Jesse said. "New delivery of books arrived today. Don't know why they didn't just bring them here," she said to Jennifer. "Billie brought them over with a load of wood and supplies, and he dropped them on the Slipper's porch. Think he plumb forgot about them," she guessed. "Bet you can find ones in the box you haven't read," she told Miles Jr.

"Thanks, Mrs. Branson." Miles Jr. quickly replaced the books he had selected back onto the shelves where he had found them. "I'll do that. Thanks a lot." He hurried toward the door, a huge smile on his face. "See you tomorrow, Mrs. Branson," he called back to Jennifer and then disappeared outside.

Jennifer grinned at Jesse. "You know you make his day every time a new box of books arrives."

Jesse shrugged. She was responsible for the large library of books Sweetwater had and it had happened quite unintentionally. A one-night stay by a traveling salesman had led to regular deliveries of books for the use of long-term guests at the Silver Slipper. But with the help of Billie, Ed, and the schoolchildren, bookshelves had been added to the schoolhouse the past summer, and the books had been moved. "I'm just happy to see someone besides us reading the dang things." She twisted around, her eyes scanning down the wall of books. "Guess it's a good thing we moved them."

Though her arms were full of her babies, Jennifer managed to reach out and place a hand on her wife's leg. "Losing them in the fire would have been disastrous." Her lessons depended heavily on the wide range of books in the school's library.

Jesse turned back around, placing a hand atop her wife's. "Fire didn't reach that part of the dining room, but I'm still glad we moved 'em. They get more use here than they ever did at the Slipper. Most travelers don't seem too interested in reading during their stay in town."

"How's the work going?"

"Good. Though it's going to take some getting used to seeing it shorter than it used to be."

In the aftermath of the fire, Jesse and Jennifer decided to make some changes at the Slipper. The fire had destroyed the end of the building that had housed the saloon, and they decided not to replace it. They rented the old general store building from Ed and moved Ruthie's dress shop into it. Luckily, other than getting a little smoky, the dresses and material had not been damaged in the fire. To Bette Mae's joy, the wall that had separated the former dress shop from the dining room was taken out and the dining room expanded. With more travelers coming through town on their way to the mining camps that kept springing up in the surrounding mountains, the Slipper's dining room had been doing standing-room-only business. The kitchen was also expanding, giving Bette Mae some additional room that she had been asking for. Neither Jesse nor Jennifer felt bad about losing the saloon business, which generally caused more trouble than it was worth. Any cowboy or drifter wanting more than a sociable drink could always go to the Oxbow, the saloon and gambling house that drew the more rough trade.

"We got the new walls raised today, and we'll be ready to start puttin' on the roof in the morning. With it being as dry as it's been, we won't have to worry about the weather giving us fits."

"It has been dry this spring. It would be nice to see some rain," Jennifer said.

"Momma," KC tilted her head back to look up at Jennifer, "we goes?"

Jennifer smiled at her daughter. "Do you want to go home, sweetie?"

"Yep." KC's head bopped up and down. "Cha-wie wants go toos."

"He does, does he?" Jennifer laughed at KC's habit of speaking for her brother. "Do you plan to ever let Charley speak for himself?"

"Nope." KC hugged her brother. "He need me do it."

"Not for long, Sunshine." Jesse laughed as she lifted the girl out of Jennifer's lap and stood her on the floor. "You too, little man," she said, gathering the baby into her arms. "Let your momma get up so we can go home." Charley giggled when Jesse placed a sloppy kiss on his cheek. "You're gonna have as much trouble gettin' in a word or two with your sister as I have with your momma."

"Jesse Marie Branson," Jennifer scolded playfully, "that's a terrible thing to tell him." She pushed the chair back away from the desk, then stood, reaching for her cane hanging on the side of her desk. She'd asked Jesse to add a peg specifically for that purpose after having to pick her cane off the floor one too many times after it had fallen from where she leaned it against a wall or her desk.

Jesse smirked. "But it's true, ain't it, Sunshine?"

"Yep," KC agreed.

"You're impossible." Jennifer laughed, tucking her arm around her wife's. "Oh, and Jesse..."

"Yes."

"Don't say—"

"AIN'T," KC shouted, finishing her mother's instruction, then bursting into giggles.

"Think you're pretty smart, don't ya?" Jesse growled at her daughter.

"Yep. Cha-wie smawt too," KC told her mommy.

"Come on." Jesse started for the door with her family. "Let's get home and let your grandparents see what little rascals you are."

"Me go see Gwumps," KC told her mothers. "Tew' 'im 'bout banging naiwes."

Jesse smiled. Her father had taken a real liking to his grandchildren. She sometimes wondered why he hadn't shown the same interest in her as a child. She realized she'd probably never know and was just glad he was better with her children. "Yeah, that'll make him real happy," she said as she followed KC outside. They stopped on the porch, giving Jennifer time to pull the door shut before they proceeded to the waiting buckboard.

"Been thinking 'bout moving the cattle up to higher pasture," Stanley Branson told Jesse as they walked out of the barn after seeing to the horses for the evening. The ranch boundaries encompassed acres of forested land, and several large mountain meadows were hidden in the trees some distance above the valley floor. The difference in elevation meant the meadows stayed cooler and the grass stayed greener long after the grasslands in the valley had dried out from lack of moisture.

Jesse swung the big barn door closed. "Mite early in the year to be doing that. We'll be needing those pastures later if we don't get rain soon."

"Grass down here is getting sparse."

Jesse looked to the sky. What few clouds she saw weren't the kind to carry much moisture. "Strange spring this has been," she said, more to herself than her father. "Don't recall ever seeing one this dry."

"Been a few I can remember. Usually didn't bode well for the rest of the year."

"Jesse?" Jennifer called from the back porch. "Are you coming? Supper's on the table."

"We're coming, darlin'," Jesse called back. "Let's give it a few more days, Poppa, before we decide anything."

"When are you and Jennifer leaving for Granite to visit that friend of yours?" Stanley asked. "If we don't move the herd before then, I'll not be able to move it on my own."

"Day after school lets out." Jesse removed her Stetson to run fingers through the tangled hair. "Maybe we should just let the herd be 'til we get back. There's plenty of grass left if we spread them out some more."

"It's your herd."

"You think they should be moved, don't you?" Jesse asked as she knocked the dirt and dust off her boots before climbing the porch steps.

Stanley cleaned his boots, too. "If it were me, I'd move 'em."

"Let's give it a few days."

"Mommy." KC was standing inside the kitchen looking out the screen door. "Huwwys."

Jesse smiled at her daughter. "We're coming, Sunshine."

"Gwumps huwwys too?"

"Yes, I'm hurrying too," Stanley grumbled. "Seems to me that there girl has more to say about what goes on around here than you do."

Jesse grinned. "Yep. Does seem like that."

"You plan on doin' anything about it?"

Jesse laughed. She knew her father adored KC and was pretending to be annoyed. "Nope."

Jesse had just slipped under the blankets and wrapped her arms around Jennifer when she heard the sound of small feet padding along the hall outside the bedroom door. She waited, knowing what would happen next; it had become a nightly ritual since the fire at the Slipper. The knob on the bedroom door turned, and the door was pushed inward. Jesse watched in the moonlight as KC walked across the room to stand beside the bed. KC had long ago become adept at climbing out of her crib.

"What ya doin' out of bed, Sunshine?" Jesse asked.

KC didn't answer. Instead, she used the arm her mommy had dropped off the side of the bed to pull herself up. She spent a few minutes finding a comfortable spot to sit, which usually ending up being on top of Jesse, like this night. Jesse waited patiently, Jennifer lying quietly at her side watching and listening.

"Mommy," KC finally said.

"Yes, Sunshine," Jesse place her arm around the girl.

"Me sca-wed."

"What are you afraid of?" Jesse asked, her voice soft.

KC sat, cocking her head off to the side like she did whenever she was thinking hard about something. "Me sca-wed Cha-wie get huwt," she finally answered.

"You mean in the fire?"

KC nodded, a sad look on her face. "I'se 'sposed ta watch him."

Jesse pulled her daughter into a hug. "Sunshine, you were watching out for him."

"He get sca-wed, Mommy," KC whimpered. "He sca-wed of smoke."

"Were you scared of the smoke?" Jesse asked as she rubbed the little girl's back soothingly. She could feel KC's head slowly move up and down in answer to her question. "But you found Charley and kept him safe, didn't you?"

"Cha-wie cwyin'." KC sniffled.

"I know. But you stayed right there, and you let me know where you were so I could find both of you, didn't you?"

"I towd Cha-wie you come." KC wiped at the tears on her face with the back of her hand. "I towd him."

"That was good, Sunshine." Jesse kissed the top of her daughter's head. "And I'll always come find you, I promise." Jesse felt the tears welling in her own eyes and didn't try to stop them when they overflowed down her cheeks. She could hear the quiet sniffling of her wife next to her. "I promise, KC," she held her daughter tight, "I'll always find you."

"I know, Mommy." KC used her mother's chest to push herself up on her arms. She leaned down and kissed Jesse. "I wuv you."

"I love you, too, Sunshine." Jesse smiled as her neck was wrapped in her daughter's arms. After a few minutes, she asked KC, "You ready to go to bed now?"

KC yawned, her fears assuaged for one more night. "Yep."

"Kiss Momma goodnight." KC shifted so she could kiss and hug Jennifer. Jesse slipped out from under the blankets. "Let's go."

KC stood, hopped to the edge of the bed, and stopped abruptly, remembering she wasn't supposed to leap into the air when Jennifer was watching. "Sa-wy," she whispered loudly to Jesse.

Jesse lifted her daughter off the bed, catching the movement of Jennifer's body under the blankets that gave away her silent laughter. "Come on. Let's get you to bed so I can come back and show your momma how much I love her."

"Ugh, Mommy," KC grumbled, her face scrounged up in annoyance. "You 'n Momma kiss too much."

"Ah, Sunshine," Jesse told her daughter as she carried her out of the room, "there's no such thing as kissing your momma too much."

When Jesse returned to the bedroom after making sure the children were tucked in, she found Jennifer still awake and waiting for her. "Thought you'd be asleep."

"Hurry up and get into bed," Jennifer ordered. "I can see from here you're cold."

Jesse smirked, the women having foregone wearing any nightshirts from almost the first night they'd made love. "You can, can you?" she snickered as she slipped under the blankets.

"Yes." Jennifer turned onto her side and cupped a warm hand over a chilled breast. "And now I have the proof of it." She flicked her thumb over the hard nipple.

"Well, now, darlin'," Jesse drawled, "you keep that up and I won't be cold for long."

"Com'ere." Jennifer's hand slipped behind Jesse's back and pulled her close. She kissed Jesse, her lips pressing tenderly against her wife's. After several heartbeats, she broke the kiss pulling back just enough so she could see into Jesse's eyes. "Do you know why I love you?"

"I lov—"

"Let me finish." Jennifer kissed Jesse again to quiet her. "When I see you talk to KC like you just did, my heart melts." Her voice was thick with the emotions she was feeling. "I don't know what I ever did to have you come into my life, but every day I'm more thankful than the day before that you're here. I don't know what I'd ever do if I lost you, Jesse. I think I'd just curl up and die."

Jesse smiled through her tears. She felt the same way about Jennifer. "I love you, too, darlin'. And to prove it…" She rolled Jennifer onto her back, flipping the blankets off their naked bodies as she did. She lowered her lips to her wife's, her hands kneading and squeezing Jennifer's breasts until erect nipples pressed against her palms. She kissed around her wife's mouth, her tongue flicking out to taste the skin her lips explored. After tasting every curve, ridge, and dip of the lips, she slipped her tongue inside, beginning her exploration all over again.

Jennifer's breathing was coming in gasps as her body reacted to her wife's loving attention. Her hands buried themselves in Jesse's hair, pulling her even closer and mashing their mouths together.

Jesse adjusted her position so she could suck a breast into her mouth, the soft flesh tasting salty on her tongue. A hand slid down Jennifer's body to her patch of silky hair, and fingers slipped into the slickness found there. Jennifer spread her legs, her hips rolling up, encouraging Jesse to enter her.

"Please, Jesse," she moaned when a hard nipple was pinched between thumb and finger. Jesse continued to slide her fingers over her wife's nether lips, pausing to circle the aroused clit on each pass, then teasing Jennifer, pressing her fingers inside and then withdrawing.

Her hands still entwined with Jesse's hair, Jennifer pulled her wife's mouth against her breast. Digging her heels into the mattress, she forced her hips off the bed, trying to draw fingers deeper inside her.

Jesse felt the increased flow of warm juices over her fingers, and Jennifer's need urged her on. She pulled her fingers free, then waited a moment before plunging them deep inside again.

Jennifer felt the fingers fill her at the same instant a thumb was pressed hard against her clit and teeth gently bit her nipple. Her head flew back and her back arched as the first wave of orgasm crashed through her. Her hips rocked in rhythm with Jesse's fingers. She clung to Jesse's head, craving the feel of her lips and tongue on her breast and nipple. A second wave engulfed her.

Jesse's fingers pressed in, pulled out, and plunged in again. With each repetition, the movement became more frantic as she felt Jennifer respond to her. She could feel her own body responding, and she pressed her sex down on Jennifer's thigh, rubbing herself up and down against the firm leg.

Jennifer felt a third wave building. She knew it would not be long until her body convulsed. "Now, Jesse!" she screamed.

Jesse thrust inside one last time, driving her fingers as deep as possible before curling them up to press against the spot that always gave Jennifer the greatest pleasure. As she felt Jennifer's release begin, she reached for her wife's leg, pulling it up hard against her own clit.

Jennifer's body jerked violently as the pent-up pleasure exploded within her.

Jesse felt her wife's release, the body convulsing beneath her, and her own release followed immediately after. She pressed her legs together, trapping her wife's thigh to keep it pressed against her clit. Her fingers were similarly trapped inside Jennifer.

It was several minutes before either woman could find the breath to speak. Jesse had collapsed on top of Jennifer, who had wrapped her in a death grip as their orgasms consumed them. Jennifer gradually released her hold on her wife, and Jesse slid off to lie at her side. She gently turned Jennifer onto her side, spooning in tight behind her. Reaching back, she grabbed hold of the blankets, pulling them over their sweaty bodies.

She whispered into her wife's ear, "I love you so much."

Jennifer entwined her fingers with Jesse's, pulling their hands to her heart, which was still beating rapidly. "I love you, Jesse Branson."

"I love you, Jennifer Branson," her wife whispered, just before sleep claimed them.

CHAPTER SIX

"Ya sure 'bout takin' them babies over the mountains again, Jesse?" Bette Mae was sitting in the shade of the awning that covered the loading dock at the back of the mercantile as she watched Jesse fill the buckboard with supplies needed for the ranch and the impending trip to Granite.

"Something wrong with taking my family to visit friends?" Jesse questioned, lifting a sack of flour off the wooden deck.

"No. It's just..."

"Just what?" Jesse stopped her work to look at her friend. She pushed the Stetson back off her brow and used her sleeve to wipe the sweat away. "Dang, it's hot," she sighed.

"Well, now, that thar's another reason ya shouldn't be takin' them babies."

Jesse cocked her head to study the older woman. "Jennifer wants to visit Leevie. You want us to leave KC and Charley with you?" she asked innocently, taking a pointed look at the children sleeping on a blanket next to Bette Mae's chair.

Bette Mae shook her head vigorously. "Heavens no! Why, she'd have the Slipper turned inside out 'fore ya was halfway outta the valley."

Jesse smirked. "Thought she was your little angel," she said, returning to the work of transferring the pile of supplies into the wagon.

"She is." Bette Mae looked down at the children. "She's jus' got more piss in her than a wolverine in a bad mood. And ya know that it's nigh impossible ta say no to that child. She's jus' so..."

"Cute?" Jesse laughed. She was well aware of how easy it was for her daughter to get her way with a simply cock of her head and a smile. It had worked on her enough times.

"Jesse, ya ain't helpin'," Bette Mae grumbled.

"All right." Jesse stopped working and hopped up to sit on the edge of the wide porch. Swiveling around, she pulled a leg up, planted her boot on the porch, then leaned back against a support post and turned her full attention to the older woman. "What's wrong, Bette Mae? Why don't you want us to take the young 'uns?"

"It's jus' that every time you go away from the valley, somethin' always seems ta happen to ya," Bette Mae explained.

Jesse could see the concern in the older woman's eyes. "Nothing is going to happen, Bette Mae. We don't have rustlers setting us up for a lynching, and there's no outlaws lying in wait to ambush us. Jennifer's father is locked away back East, and Harrington hasn't been heard from since he left town. There's nothing to worry about."

"There's always somethin' when ye're involved, Jesse. I don' want any of ya ta get hurt."

"We won't." Jesse stood and went over to Bette Mae. "I promise that I won't let anything happen to any of us." She leaned over to place a quick kiss on her temple. "Besides," she said as she straightened up, "Jennifer has you beat in the worrying department, and she won't let me take any chances this time. She's made me promise that if we run into trouble…*any* trouble," she emphasized, "we high-tail it back home."

"Lordy," Bette Mae smiled, "at least one of yas has some sense. What about the ranch? Yer poppa can't handle it alone."

"And why not?" Stanley walked out from the back of the store and glowered at Bette Mae. "I'm not dead yet."

"Get what you needed, Poppa?" Jesse asked.

"Yep. Ed had some real nice ones," Stanley held up a pair of new axes. "These should make short work of cuttin' firewood." He winked at Jesse. "Told him to put it on the Slipper's account, I did."

"The Slipper's account!" Bette Mae exclaimed, swallowing the bait. "Now why would ya go and do a fool thing like that? Ya know full well I ain't gonna buy no new axe. Why, the cost of it would probably pay for a week's worth a' flour. And the Slipper needs flour a hell of a lot more than it needs ta pay fer yer toys."

"Ain't a toy, Bette Mae." Jesse defended her father's purchase. "Axe I've been using out at the ranch is getting too worn to keep sharp — hard to cut firewood with a dull axe. And we've got to cut back some willows down by the river. With the river getting so low, cattle are having a rough time getting through them. Had to free up two that got tangled in there this week alone."

"Why ain't ya movin' 'em up high, then?" Bette Mae asked.

"That there is a mighty good question." Stanley added his purchases to the back of the buckboard. "Been asking her that myself for the past few weeks."

Jesse knew it would be easier on the cattle to move them, but some instinct deep inside her was telling her not to. "Not sure why, I just know it isn't the best idea," she told the others. "It may be a little hard on the herd to stay put, but that's what they're gonna do." She scratched the back of her head, hoping that saying the words aloud would make them come true. "Weather is bound to break soon." The sound of KC waking drew her attention. "Poppa, can you get the rest of this in the wagon? I need to see to KC and Charley."

"Yep." Stanley was already lifting the last box of foodstuffs over the side of the wagon.

KC sat up, rubbing her eyes. "Mommy, I hungwy," she mumbled.

Bette Mae laughed, a hearty, joyful laugh that floated on the dry air. "When ain't ya, child? When ain't ya?"

Hearing the familiar voice, KC twisted her head around to look for its owner. "Hi, 'Ette," she said, smiling brightly.

"That," Bette Mae pointed at the child, "is wha' I was talkin' 'bout. How do ya say no ta that?"

"Ya don't," Stanley grumbled.

KC turned at her grandfather's voice. "Hi, Gwumps. You hungwy too?"

"Oh, no you don't." Jesse knelt down beside the blanket. "We don't have time for you to work your magic to get some treats. We need to get Charley up and changed and get over to the schoolhouse to pick up your momma. Today's the last day of school, and she's gonna be in a big hurry to get home."

KC's face fell at her mother's words. "No tweats," she pouted, her lower lip quivering.

"Did I hear someone say treats?" Thaddeus Newby, owner and editor of the town newspaper, walked out from the back of the store carrying a handful of freshly baked cookies. "I was over having lunch at the Slipper, and I just couldn't leave without some of these. Fresh from the oven, too." He bent down and handed one of the cookies to KC. Placing a second cookie on the blanket near Jesse, he said, "This one's for Charley when he wakes up." He passed the remaining cookies to Stanley and Bette Mae.

"T'anks." KC's pout disappeared as she grabbed the still-warm cookie and broke off a piece. She held the bite out for Jesse while she bit off a piece for herself. "Goods. You eat." She grinned as she chewed.

Jesse opened her mouth wide to gather in her daughter's fingers along with the offered bite. "You're right," she teased, "you do taste good. The cookie isn't bad, either."

"You si-wy." KC giggled, shoving the rest of the treat into her mouth, then held her hand up to Thaddeus. "Mo-we, pease."

Jesse grabbed the hand and placed it back in KC's lap. "Nope, Sunshine, that's all you get." Charley's eyes popped open, and the baby smiled at his mother. "Hi there, little man." Jesse tickled his tummy. "Did you smell that cookie?" She laughed as Charley giggled.

Charley rolled over onto his stomach and then pushed himself up on all fours. He crawled to Jesse, plopped down to sit next to her, and waited.

"How come your sister isn't as well behaved?" Jesse chuckled, bending over to kiss the baby's head. She picked up the cookie and broke it in half. "Here ya go." She handed a half to Charley. "Should we keep this piece for Momma?"

Charley smiled around a mouthful of cookie. KC stood beside Jesse. "Cha-wie says okay, Mommy."

"Lordy, tha' poor child ain't never gonna learn ta talk," Bette Mae said.

KC patted Jesse's shoulder. "Mommy."

"What is it, Sunshine?"

KC leaned in close and whispered, "'Ette say ain't."

Jesse nodded. "That she did. But I think that's all right. Your momma just doesn't want you or me to say it."

"Oh." KC peeked around Jesse to look at Bette Mae. "It okay," she informed the woman.

Bette Mae laughed, opening her arms wide. "Come here, child." Giggling, KC ran for Bette Mae and was wrapped up in the woman's arms. "Ya take real good care of yer momma and mommy, ya hear?" Bette Mae hugged the girl tight. "I don't want nothin' happenin' ta them."

"Okay," KC agreed.

"Leaving for Granite in the morning, Jesse?" Thaddeus asked.

"No." Jesse laid Charley on the blanket so she could change his britches. "Have a few things to take care of out at the ranch first. Probably first of the week."

"Too bad you're not taking a wagon," Ed said, walking out of the store. "I have a package for a young couple in Philipsburg." The mining camp of Granite was located a few miles up the mountain from the larger town. "You could make some money out of the trip."

"What's in it?"

"Dresses."

"Why'd they order those from you?" Thaddeus asked. "I'm sure there must be a dress shop or two in Philipsburg?"

"They were passing through a few weeks back and stopped in Ruthie's shop. Ordered the dresses and I agreed to get them delivered when they were ready."

"Couple of dresses can't take up much room," Jesse said. "Guess we could add them to one of the packs."

"Don't want to put you out none," Ed said, hoping Jesse would not be dissuaded.

"You're not. We'll take them with us."

"Thanks, Jesse. I'll be right back." The storekeeper disappeared back into the building.

"There ya go, Charley." Jesse pulled the baby into her arms. "All fresh and clean for Momma." She carried the boy to the wagon and handed him up to his grandfather, who was already sitting on the wagon bench. "Come on, KC."

KC gave Bette Mae a peck on the cheek, then dropped out of her lap and ran toward her mother. Not hesitating when she reached the edge of the platform, she flew into the air.

Jesse turned just in time. "Whoa there, Sunshine." Jesse snatched her daughter out of the air. "You need to make sure I'm ready for ya."

"You weady, Momma." KC wrapped her arms around Jesse's neck. "You a'ways weady."

"With you around, smart britches," Stanley grumbled, accepting the child from Jesse and sitting her in his lap with Charley, "she ain't got much of a choice."

Bette Mae chuckled. "Ain't that the truth."

"Here you go, Jesse," Ed said, coming out of the store. "It's not too big a package, is it?"

"Nope." Jesse took the bundle wrapped in brown paper and tied neatly with a piece of string.

Glad to have his problem solved, Ed smiled. He didn't have many deliveries to Philipsburg; it was a big enough town to have freight delivered directly to it. If Jesse hadn't agreed to carry the package, he wasn't sure how long it would have been before he managed to get it delivered. "I wrote their name on the paper and where they said they could be found."

"Have a good trip, Jesse," Thaddeus said as the rancher placed the package into the wagon, tucking it into a box to protect it on the trip to the ranch.

"We will. You folks make sure to keep an eye on Ruthie and the baby. Jennifer doesn't want Ruthie working too much right now."

"I'll make sure Billie spends as much time with her as he can," Ed added.

Bette Mae walked to the edge of the platform and stood between Ed and Thaddeus. "Be careful."

"We will." Jesse climbed up onto the wagon seat. Unwrapping Boy's reins from the brake handle, she used her booted foot to release the brake. With a flick of her wrist, the reins slapped on the broad back of the work horse, and he took a few steps forward, straining against the weight of the wagon until the wheels began to turn.

"Bye, 'Ette." KC squirmed out of Stanley's grasp and knelt between her mother and grandfather, facing backward on the wagon seat. With one hand holding tight on the back of the seat, she waved to her friends with the other. "Bye. T'anks for da cookie."

Bette Mae waved back, wiping a tear from her cheek. "Bye, li'l angel."

After checking on the horses and making sure they were settled for the night, Jesse pulled the barn doors shut. She walked across the ranch yard looking up at the night sky, unsurprised to see it free of clouds. Stars twinkled brightly and made her smile. On evenings like this one, she always thought of the first few nights she and Jennifer had spent together, camping out under the stars and falling in love. Thinking of her wife made her want to get back to the house where she would find the woman that had become everything to her; she quickened her steps.

Jennifer was waiting for Jesse in the swing on the back porch. "Hi."

"Whatcha doin' out here, darlin'?" Jesse asked.

Jennifer smiled. "Waiting for the woman I love."

Jesse smirked as she walked over to the swing. "You expecting her soon, or can I snuggle up with you until she gets here?"

Jennifer looked up at her wife seductively, patting the swing beside her. "That depends."

"On what?" Jesse asked as she took the offered seat.

"On how good you snuggle." Jennifer nestled against Jesse, sighing happily when strong arms wrapped around her.

"Well," Jesse drawled, pulling her wife close, "I've had lots of lessons from the best snuggler ever, so I'm thinking I can do a right fair job of it."

"Oh?" Jennifer snuggled into Jesse's embrace. "And who would that be?"

"A little ginger-haired spitfire if ever there was one," Jesse teased. "I think you might even know her."

"Really?"

"Yep."

"Does she have a name?"
"Yep. Might pretty one, too."
"Care to share?"
"Sure."
"Well?"

Jesse turned her head and placed a tender kiss on the tip of Jennifer's nose. "I'm surprised you don't know, darlin'." She grinned, pressing her forehead against Jennifer's. "Her name is KC."

Jennifer playfully slapped Jesse's belly. "Bad."

"I love you." Jesse leaned in just enough to press her lips against her wife's. She took her time exploring the soft skin with her lips and tongue.

Jennifer moaned, her eyes sliding closed as her wife's love spread throughout her body. "That was nice," she sighed when Jesse took a moment to breathe.

"It certainly was." Jesse was so close to Jennifer that she could taste the air her lover exhaled.

Jennifer's eyes slowly opened to look into Jesse's. "I love you."

Leaning back on the swing, Jesse pulled Jennifer with her and braced her foot on the porch. "What about that woman you said you was waiting for?" she asked, pumping her leg slightly to start a gentle motion of the swing beneath them.

"What woman?" Jennifer laid her head against Jesse's shoulder, content in the closeness of her wife and the soothing motion of the swing.

Jesse chuckled. "Forgot her already, did ya?"

"Nope." Jennifer started unbuttoning Jesse's shirt. "Just found somebody I like a whole lot better." She slipped her hand inside the flannel shirt to rest it on the warm skin hidden beneath.

The women sat like that for several minutes. No words were necessary as they savored the peaceful night, the starlit sky, and each other.

"So, you planning on telling me why you were sitting out here all alone?" Jesse murmured in Jennifer's ear. The swing had been well used since she'd hung it weeks earlier as a surprise for her wife. But almost always, Jennifer had the children with her or the two of them would sit in it after the children had been put to bed.

"I was just thinking…" Jennifer's hand began to creep up toward the firm breasts she loved to hold.

Jesse felt her heart race. "'Bout what?"

Jennifer's hand stilled. She wanted to tease Jesse, but she also wanted a little time to think about her answer. Should she tell

Jesse why she wanted to see Leevie? She didn't want Jesse to try and talk her out of the decision she had made some time earlier, but was it fair to wait and spring it on her after they arrived in Granite? Then again, would Jesse even care? The sound of feet padding across the kitchen floor and someone leaning against the screen door disrupted her thoughts.

"Didn't you put them to bed?" Jesse whispered.

"Yes," Jennifer whispered back. "Didn't you tell her she wasn't supposed to climb down the stairs alone?"

"Yep."

"You sure it's her?"

"It sure ain't Charley," Jesse grumbled. Without moving, she addressed her daughter. "Sunshine, are you out of bed?"

"Yep," KC said through the screen door.

"Didn't Momma tell you to go to sleep?"

"Yep."

"Then why are you up?"

Jesse and Jennifer heard the screen door squeak slightly as it was slowly pushed open. Small feet padded across the wood planks on the porch until their sleepy-eyed daughter stood in front of them, cocking her head to the side to study them.

"I ti-wed," KC told her mothers, one hand balled into a fist to rub her eyes.

Jesse fought the laugh threatening to come out. With hair sticking out in every which direction, their daughter looked just like Jennifer when she woke in the morning. "That's why your momma put you to bed."

Jennifer sat up, pulling her hand out of Jesse's shirt. She laughed when her love groaned in protest over the action. "Sweetie," she bent down to KC, "why did you get out of bed if you're tired?" When KC moved into her arms she lifted her daughter into her lap.

KC looked up at Jennifer, her face sad. "Miss Mommy."

"What do you mean, you miss me?" Jesse asked. "I'm right here."

"I think," Jennifer told Jesse, "that she means she missed you saying goodnight to her. Isn't that right, sweetie?" she asked. "Did you and Charley miss Mommy's kisses tonight?"

KC nodded, her lower lip poking out as she looked up at Jesse. "Yep."

Jesse smiled at her daughter. "I guess I better fix that, huh?" KC waited expectantly. "Come on, Sunshine." She held her arms open. "Let's go put you to bed properly."

KC scrambled into her mother's arms, giggling happily when Jesse smothered her with kisses.

Jesse stood, holding a hand out to Jennifer. "Shall we put this young 'un to bed, darlin'?"

"I think that would be best." Jennifer let Jesse pull her out of the swing.

"Is your brother awake, too?" Jesse asked as she and Jennifer walked hand-in-hand to the door.

"Nope. Cha-wie seeping," KC told her mothers.

"Oh, so he doesn't need me to kiss him goodnight," Jesse pouted.

KC patted her mommy's cheek. "He just a baby, Mommy."

"And you're not?" Jesse held the screen door open for Jennifer.

"Nope." KC beamed. "I big."

"Not that big," Jesse snickered, tickling her. "You still need your mommy to kiss you goodnight."

"Jesse, stop it," Jennifer warned when KC let loose a flood of giggles. "You'll wake up Charley."

"Sorry, darlin'." Jesse stopped agitating KC. "Settle down, Sunshine," she told the girl, "so I can help your momma upstairs."

"Okay." KC settled immediately. She knew how difficult it was for her mother to climb stairs.

Jennifer slipped her arm around Jesse's, taking advantage of her wife's strength to help pull her damaged leg up each step. It took several moments to reach the top landing but, as usual, Jesse took every step with her, never showing any impatience.

The women carried KC down the hall to the children's bedroom and slipped inside to find Charley sitting up in his crib.

"Hey, little man." Jennifer limped to the baby's crib and leaned over the railing to kiss her son. "Are you waiting for Mommy to kiss you goodnight, too?"

Charley smiled at his momma and started to chatter in gibberish. "Cha-wie say yep," KC told Jesse as she was placed down in her own crib.

"That's an awful lot for him to be saying if all he said was *yep*." Jesse tucked the blanket around KC. She bent over and kissed the girl's cheek. "Good night, Sunshine. You go to sleep now, okay?"

KC yawned. "Okay."

Jesse switched places with Jennifer. She bent over the side of the crib to check the blanket Jennifer had tucked around the baby and kiss her son. "Good night, Charley." He reached up, pressing his tiny hand against his mother's cheek. Jesse felt the tears welling in her eyes and brushed them away before they had a chance to fall. "I love you, too," she whispered.

CHAPTER SEVEN

Jesse tightened one of the straps that bound the packs to Boy. "That should do it, darlin'."

Jennifer stood on the back porch of the house; for the past couple of days, that was where they had placed the items they would take with them to Granite. "It doesn't look like we forgot anything."

"We goes?" KC asked.

She and Charley were sitting in the porch swing watching their mothers work. Her mothers had quite accidentally discovered the little girl couldn't get out of the swing on her own, which made it perfect for keeping track of their easily distracted daughter.

Jesse smiled at her daughter. "Pretty soon, Sunshine. First we need to check Charley's britches and say goodbye to your grandma and grandpa."

KC slapped her hands against her thighs in frustration. She was anxious to get going since she liked to ride Dusty with her mommy.

"Where are Marie and Stanley?" Jennifer asked, surprised Jesse's parents had yet to appear from their cabin. The sun had been up for a couple of hours, and they had been told the women were leaving right after breakfast. "I'd expected them to eat with us this morning."

"Don't know," Jesse said, making a final check of the straps and bindings. "I'll walk over and check soon as I get Charley changed."

"Why don't you and KC do that while I take care of Charley?" Jennifer offered, as anxious to get moving as her antsy daughter was.

"You sure?"

"Yes, go ahead."

"All right." Jesse stepped up onto the porch and wrapped her arms around Jennifer, hugging her tight. "We won't be long, darlin'."

Jennifer leaned into her wife's embrace. "Just bring them back with you; I want to know they're okay."

Stanley Branson rounded the corner of the house, his wife right behind him. "Good, we caught you. Marie was afraid you might already be on your way."

Jesse smiled at her parents. "You know we wouldn't leave without saying goodbye, Poppa. KC and I were just fixin' to come look for you. Where have you been?"

Stanley helped his wife up onto the porch. "Your momma is feeling poorly this morning. She didn't want you to be worrying 'bout her. Took me this long just ta talk her into coming over and saying goodbye. I told her the young 'uns would be expecting us."

"Gwumps," KC called out, her hands held high in anticipation of being set free from the swing.

"You're not feeling well, Marie?" Jennifer asked as she picked Charley up from the swing, not wanting the baby sitting in it alone.

Jesse crossed the porch to where her mother was standing. "Maybe we should hold off going for a few days, Mom."

Marie patted Jesse on the arm. "Nonsense. It's just a woman thing," she whispered. "Your poppa has never understood those things."

"You sure, Mom?"

"Course I'm sure. You go on with your plans." Marie smiled to reassure her daughter. "I'll be just fine in a day or two."

Jesse was torn. She knew Jennifer was anxious to get to Granite, but she was concerned about her mother. Marie had never been a strong person, and she worried anytime the older woman didn't feel well.

"We can wait a few days, Jesse," Jennifer said, carrying Charley over to join the others.

"No," Marie insisted. "I'll be fine. I just need to take it easy for a day or two."

Jesse wasn't convinced. "I don't know, Mom. If it's all right with Jennifer, I think we should stay put, at least until you're feeling better."

Marie bristled. "Jesse Marie Branson, you will do no such thing. I said I'll be fine and I will. Now you take your wife and your young 'uns to Granite like they're expecting you to do," she said in a sharp tone.

"And they say I'm the stubborn one," Stanley whispered to KC, who giggled.

"All right, if you're sure," Jesse rubbed her cheeks, trying to hide the humiliation she was feeling over her mother's rebuke. "Let me take care of Charley, then we'll go." Jesse snatched the baby from Jennifer and hurried into the house.

Jennifer watched the screen door bounce against the door frame behind Jesse. "I think I should go check on her," she told her in-laws. "You be good, KC. Mommy and I will be right back. Okay?" KC nodded, her face sad as she watched Jennifer disappear inside.

Stanley turned to his wife. "What the blazes was that all about?"

"Mommy sad," KC said.

"What for?" Stanley grumbled.

KC laid her head on her grandfather's shoulder, her eyes glued to the screen door.

Marie looked at the child, and a flood of memories flashed through her mind, memories of a small girl who could do no right, it seemed. She wondered how much hurt her daughter still carried inside her. "I think I should go see to Jesse," she told Stanley. "I'm afraid I may have hurt her feelings."

Stanley slumped down on the swing. He had his own memories of his daughter's childhood, and not many of them made him proud. But he was proud of the woman she had grown into and the daughter she was to him now. If anyone could ease Jesse's unforgotten pain it would be her wife. "Wait. Leave 'em be." Marie nodded and joined her husband on the swing.

"Jesse?" Jennifer called softly as she tapped on the door to the children's bedroom.

Jesse grabbed a chair, placing it next to Jennifer for her to sit. "You didn't need to come up here, darlin'. That's a lot of strain on your leg just before we leave."

"That's okay." Jennifer limped past the chair and wrapped her arms around her wife. "You all right?"

Jesse twisted her head to smile at her wife. "Guess I made a fool of myself down there, huh?"

"No." Jennifer continued to hold Jesse as she finished dressing Charley. "Want to talk about it?"

"Not much to talk about. Just haven't heard Mom use that tone in some time." Jesse lifted the baby into her arms and turned to face her wife. "Made me feel like I was that little girl all over again." She wrapped her free arm around Jennifer. "The one that always tried so hard to please them but never could."

"That's not who you are now, sweetheart." Jennifer leaned into Jesse. "It's not who they are, either."

Jesse kissed Jennifer's forehead. "I know. It just caught me off guard, that's all."

"You sure?"

"Yep. I'm fine. Let's go get our daughter and say our goodbyes."

Jennifer leaned back just enough to look into Jesse's eyes. "I love you, Jesse Marie Branson."

"I love you too, darlin'," Jesse bent forward to capture her wife's lips in a tender kiss.

"Bleck," Charley snorted.

Both women looked at their son. "Is that a word?" Jesse asked.

"I don't know," Jennifer stared at her son. "I hope not. I'd hate to think that was the first thing he said."

"I don't know, darlin'. Seems if I remember right, KC's first word was *moo*."

"That doesn't mean I want Charley's to be *bleck*."

Jesse chuckled. "Come on. Let's get downstairs before KC talks them into coming up here." Jesse bent forward again. As their lips touched, Charley voiced his opinion again.

"Bleck," he said, scrunching up his nose and shaking his head.

Jesse stared at the baby. "Oh, boy. We are really going to have to keep you away from your sister."

"You have a good trip." Stanley was standing beside Dusty. Jesse sat in the saddle with KC in front of her. "And don't you be frettin' about the ranch. It'll be here when you get back, I promise."

His pledge wasn't an idle one. He knew the last time Jesse and Jennifer had left the ranch for a period of time, they had come back to a burned-out shell of rubble instead of the home they loved. He was determined that would not happen again, not on his watch.

"Thanks, Poppa," Jesse offered her hand to her father. "I know you'll take care of the place."

Stanley grasped the outstretched hand. "I will, daughter."

"Bye, Gwumps." KC grinned, her little hand waving enthusiastically. "Bye, Gwamma."

"Goodbye, smart britches." Stanley reached up to tickle his granddaughter. "You be good, you hear."

KC giggled. "I good, Gwumps."

Marie had apologized to her daughter, but she could see the hurt still reflected in Jesse's eyes. "You'll watch out for her, won't you?" she said to Jennifer, who was mounted on Blaze.

"I will, Marie," Jennifer said, repositioning the carry sack on her back where Charley sat. "She'll be fine." She smiled down at her mother-in-law. "Really."

Marie smiled back. If there was one person to entrust her daughter's feelings to, it was Jennifer, and she knew it. "Be safe," she whispered.

"We will." Jennifer nudged Blaze up beside Dusty. "Ready, sweetheart?"

Jesse grinned. "Just waiting for you, darlin'."

"Well, then, let's get going."

Jesse ruffled her daughter's hair. "Okay, Sunshine, Momma says it's time to go."

"Gid-diup, Dusty!" KC yelled, tapping her heels on the horse's sides. Dusty raised her head, shaking it, then twisted her neck to look back at the miniature rider giving the commands.

Jesse laughed. "Better get used to it, girl. Won't be long before she's running the whole show." She tightened her grip on Boy's reins and flicked her wrist to set Dusty in motion. The golden horse stepped forward a few steps.

Not happy with the palomino's speed, KC again yelled, "Gid-diup!" encouraging Dusty to move faster.

"Best let her set the pace, Sunshine," Jesse said, stilling the girl's legs as she repeatedly tapped them against the horse's sides. "We don't want her to get mad and make us walk all the way to Granite." KC frowned but said nothing. Dusty quickened her pace to a slow trot as soon as KC quit trying to make her do it. "Don't know which one of you is worse," Jesse teased, then twisted in the saddle to address her parents. "You be sure and send for Bette Mae if you don't feel better tomorrow," she called to her mother.

"You just worry about yourselves; I'll be fine."

Jennifer waved as they rode around the corral fence and headed south. "Goodbye."

Jesse glanced skyward. The sun was almost straight up. "Bit later than we were expecting to leave."

Jennifer laughed. "It seems we have a bit more to get ready now."

"That it does." Jesse chuckled. "Well, gid-diup, Dusty. We've got some ground to make up." The mare snorted and then picked up the pace.

KC clapped her hands, happy to finally be moving fast enough for the wind to rustle her hair. "Cha-wie," she called to her brother, "dis fun."

"Bleck."

"I've missed this," Jennifer said, stirring a pot of soup. She was sitting on a stool Jesse had fashioned out of a piece of canvas and some legs from an old chair. The stool provided her a comfortable way to sit in front of the fire without having to kneel on her bad leg, and when she wasn't using it, it collapsed into a neat bundle for packing.

"Missed what?" Jesse paused in her task of setting up the camp to look at her wife. "Cooking? You do that every night, darlin'." She went back to sorting through their packs and pulled out their bedrolls and blankets.

Jennifer grinned. "No, silly, I missed being out like this. Just us."

"Ain't just us anymore, darlin'," Jesse said, carrying the bedrolls into the tent where she spread them out on the canvas floor.

Jennifer turned her head to check on KC and Charley playing on a blanket near the fire. "It's just us, sweetheart. Only now, it's more of us."

Jesse smiled as she stepped back out of the tent. "Last time we used this tent, they both slept in empty pack boxes. Don't think we'd get them to do that now."

"No, I doubt we would. Do you need help, sweetheart?"

"Nope, almost done. You just stay put and rest that leg. After we feed them and get them to bed, I'll give you a nice rubdown, just like before."

"I don't think we'll have much trouble getting them to sleep tonight." Jennifer watched KC rubbing her eyes.

Jesse grinned. "Nothing like riding on the back of a horse all day to tucker out young 'uns. Do you want to give them a bath tonight?" Jesse knelt beside Jennifer and placed a hand on her wife's thigh, gently squeezing it.

"No. I don't think they'll stay awake long enough for that. Soup is ready. Will you get Charley?"

"Sure," Jesse said, but she stayed where she was.

Jennifer looked into Jesse's eyes and smiled at the love she saw in them.

"Have I ever told you how pretty you are?" Jesse's voice was low and husky.

"A time or two."

"Not enough. I should tell you every day." Jesse leaned forward until her forehead was resting against her wife's. "Jennifer Branson, you are the prettiest girl I have ever seen. And I love you so much I think sometimes my heart is gonna just burst."

Jennifer smiled. "Jesse, I think you are the most romantic person I've ever met. Now, go get the babies so we can feed them and put them to bed. I want to show you just how much I love you."

"Yes, ma'am." Jesse leapt to her feet. "Come on, you rascals," she growled playfully. "You've got to be eating your supper, and quick. Your momma wants to show me something."

"Me see, Mommy?" KC asked as Jesse scooped her and Charley into her arms.

"Nope, Sunshine." Jesse buried her face into KC's belly, causing the babies to giggle uncontrollably.

Jennifer shook her head, resigned to her wife's playful behavior. "Jesse, why do you always have to stir them up just before bedtime?"

"'Cause it's so much fun." Jesse sat down on the ground next to Jennifer. She propped KC up in her lap and handed Charley up to his momma. "And 'cause I love them."

"You're impossible." Jennifer laughed, handing a bowl of warmed soup to her wife.

"And you still love me." Jesse accepted the bowl and held it for KC to dip a spoon into. She kept a close watch on the girl as they shared the soup.

"Yes, improbable as it seems, I do love you." Jennifer held a spoonful of cooled soup to Charley's mouth, letting the baby swallow it in his own time. "Jesse, will we take the same pass over the mountain as before?"

"Nope." Jesse refilled the bowl from the pot simmering over the fire. "We won't go as far south as before. We'll cut across a pass just this side of the badlands."

"What's that way like?"

"First part of the trail follows a creek to a nice little waterfall, then it leaves the creek for a few miles as it climbs up to the pass, where we'll go by a couple of small lakes before picking up another creek flowing the other way. We'll be in trees most of the way, so that should help with the hot days."

"It sounds nice."

"It is. When we drop down out of the trees, we'll be in a pretty little valley with a creek running right through the center of it."

"Is that where Philipsburg is?"

"No, but it's not much further. We'll climb out of that valley over a range of hills and drop down into the next valley. Philipsburg is there, across the valley from where we'll drop over the pass."

"Is it good trail?" Jennifer asked.

"You worried about the young 'uns?"

"Yes. I remember how restless KC got when we rode back from Bannack. But, I'm also not sure…"

"You'll do fine, darlin'. Most of the way we'll be setting our own trail, but we shouldn't have any trouble like last time. And there'll be plenty of spots to stop and rest whenever we want. We don't have to worry about how far to travel each day, we'll just set our own pace to Philipsburg. And once we get there, we just have to ride up the wagon road to Granite."

"How long do you think it'll take?"

"Quickest we can make it is two days, but we can take as long as you like."

Jennifer silently considered the possibilities. *I want to get to Granite and talk to Leevie, but having time with Jesse and the children is also something I want. And need. I guess we'll just take it day by day. Either way, I really can't lose.*

"Darlin'," Jesse said quietly. "I think your soup has put this one to sleep."

Jennifer looked down to see KC sound asleep, her head lolled back and resting on Jesse's arm.

Jesse gently cradled the sleeping girl in her arms as she stood. "I'll put her to bed, then come back and get him." She nodded to the baby half asleep in Jennifer's lap.

"How's that feel?" Jesse asked.

"Wonderful," Jennifer sighed. Wearing only her shirt, she was lying on her stomach on a blanket next to the fire. Jesse was straddling her legs, massaging the soreness out of her impaired one.

As she worked her fingers into tight thigh muscles, Jesse's hands roamed a little further up Jennifer's legs, her wife's quiet moans encouraging her to continue.

Jennifer felt Jesse's hands move closer to the apex of her legs, and she felt a surge of heat burst from around her clit and spread up her belly. "Jesse, you keep that up and…"

"And what, darlin'?" Jesse purred.

"And…" Jennifer rolled over, surprising her wife with the sudden movement. "And I'm just going to have to do this." She grabbed hold of Jesse's shirt, pulling her down on top of her. Her other hand slipped up her wife's back until it reached her neck, and she pulled Jesse to her. Jennifer's mouth was open when their lips met, and she didn't have to wait long for Jesse's tongue to enter it. Wrapping her tongue around her wife's, she pressed their mouths together in a searing kiss.

"Wow," Jesse breathed when their lips parted moments later.

Jennifer grinned, pulling Jesse's shirt free of her pants. "There's more where that came from."

"Darlin'?" Jesse lifted herself up, aiding her wife in undressing her. "Don't you want to go into the tent?"

"No." Jennifer worked at the buttons of Jesse's shirt. "I don't want to move. I want to make love to you right here."

"Okay." Jesse grinned as Jennifer leaned up to latch onto a bared nipple. As the warm lips sucked on her tender flesh, a jolt of heat exploded in her groin. There was no stopping. She pressed her hand over Jennifer's patch of silky hair, the heat she felt there matching her own.

"No," Jennifer said in a soft voice, reaching down to still Jesse's hand. "I want to make love to *you*. Change places with me."

As Jesse did as she was asked, Jennifer straddled Jesse's waist and finished undoing the buttons on her shirt. She pushed the fabric over Jesse's shoulders, then, cupping her hands around each breast, she gently squeezed the firm tissue. The nipples hardened, and she rolled them between her thumb and finger, applying a little more pressure with each touch.

"Ahhhhhh," Jesse groaned. She tried to reach for her wife, but the shirt, pushed only part way down her arms, prevented her from doing so.

Jennifer smiled. "Tonight, you're mine," she whispered, leaning down to press her lips against her wife's. As she deepened the kiss, her tongue slid into Jesse's mouth. She reached between their bodies to the buttons on Jesse's pants. Once the pants were loose, she slipped a hand inside, her fingers exploring the pulsing clit and surrounding wetness.

Jesse moaned, her hips rising to meet Jennifer's hand. "Not yet, sweetheart," Jennifer whispered, pulling her hand away from Jesse's heated center. Placing both hands on Jesse's hips, she slowly pushed herself up until she was straddling her wife's thighs. She rose up on her knees, pushing the pants down Jesse's long legs until they could go no further because of her boots. Gently easing Jesse's knees apart, she pushed them up until they were parallel to her hips.

What she had in mind would be awkward because Jesse still had her boots on and her pants were bunched around her ankles, but Jennifer didn't care. Tonight she would show her wife just how much she loved her.

"Jennifer?" Jesse's voice shook with desire as she watched her wife position herself between her legs.

"Shhh." Jennifer smiled at Jesse. "I love you," she murmured, lowering her mouth onto the throbbing clit.

Jesse thought her head was exploding. It flew back against the blanket as a scream escaped her lips. Unable to move her arms, she balled her fists into the blanket. Her chest was rising and falling at a speed that matched her racing heart. She had never felt anything like the rush of ecstasy from Jennifer's lips on her clit.

Jesse's hips were bucking, making it difficult for Jennifer to maintain contact with the hard bundle of nerves. She pulled back, giving her lover time to relax. When Jesse sank back onto the blanket, Jennifer resumed her attack. Only now, instead of concentrating on Jesse's clit, she slowly kissed and licked her way to the center of her wife's need.

Jesse groaned, her breath coming in short bursts as her orgasm began to build.

Jennifer plunged her tongue as far inside her wife as she could. She enjoyed the smooth, silky texture of the overheated tissue she found inside, and she let her tongue roam freely over it.

Jesse screamed and bucked as waves of molten lava crashed through her body. Her muscles instinctively clamped down on Jennifer's tongue, trying to draw it deeper inside her.

Her mouth mashed against her wife's wet, throbbing sex, Jennifer was lost in the new sensations she was tasting and feeling. She felt her own need building as she tried to force her tongue further inside. Her hand moved up to Jesse's clit, and she pressed her thumb hard against the bundle.

Jesse's orgasm exploded inside her. Hips convulsing uncontrollably, she forced her sex against her wife's mouth, intensifying the sensations. So lost in her own pleasure was she that she didn't feel Jennifer's body begin to shudder or hear her wife's screams of pleasure.

"Darlin'?" Jesse croaked, her throat so dry she could barely force the word out.

Jennifer was sprawled between Jesse's legs, too exhausted to move. "Hmmm?"

"Darlin?" Jesse tried again. She wanted to hold her wife in her arms, but she couldn't raise them and couldn't remember why. "I need you," she managed to choke out.

Hearing the frustration in Jesse's voice, Jennifer pushed up on her elbows to look at her. "Are you okay?" she asked, concerned she might have done something to hurt her wife.

"No." Jesse lifted her head just enough to look at Jennifer. "I need to hold you." Jennifer crawled up Jesse's body. "My arms," Jesse told her. "Free my arms."

"I'll try." Jennifer studied the situation and saw that she could not remove the shirt without Jesse's help. "You're going to have to sit up." She grabbed hold of Jesse's shoulders.

With both women summoning what strength they had left, they managed to get the shirt off. Free to move her arms, Jesse wrapped them around Jennifer as she collapsed back on the blanket.

"That was the... Well, I've got to tell you... Damn, Jennifer..." Jesse hugged Jennifer. "That was really somethin'."

"It was, wasn't it?"

"Yes, ma'am, it surely was." Jesse rolled her head to kiss Jennifer. "Ready for bed?"

"Oh, yes. I don't think KC and Charley will be the only ones not having trouble sleeping tonight."

"Probably not." Jesse slipped out from under Jennifer. It took some effort, but she managed to stand on her shaky legs and pull her pants back up and fasten them. "Come on," she reached down for Jennifer. Once Jennifer was standing, Jesse scooped her into her arms and carried her to the tent.

CHAPTER EIGHT

Jesse slowly lifted her eyelids, astounded that the night had passed so quickly. She remembered nothing after carrying Jennifer into the tent and crawling into their bedroll. *Course, after what you did to me last night, darlin', that ain't too surprising.* She chuckled softly at the sleeping woman draped over her. Rolling her head to check on the children, she saw KC sitting up in her bedroll, watching her.

"Hi," KC whispered, a smile spreading across her face.

"Morning, Sunshine," Jesse whispered back. "Is Charley still sleeping?"

"Yep. Just wike Momma?"

"Don't suppose I can get you to go back to sleep?" Jesse asked, wanting to stay in bed and snuggle with her wife.

"Nope."

Jesse smiled. KC, an early riser, was always full of energy for the coming day as soon as her eyes popped open. She wasn't upset with KC's response, many mornings she'd ask the girl to go back to sleep, and she would. So if today wasn't one of those, it was okay. She eased out from under Jennifer, doing her best not to wake her wife. She slipped out of the bedroll, then tucked it in around her wife so she'd stay warm in the morning coolness. She moved over to the bedroll where the children had spent the night. Carefully, she lifted Charley out from under the blanket and carried the sleeping baby over to tuck him in with Jennifer.

Even asleep, Jennifer sensed the baby's presence. She turned onto her side, stretching a protective hand over the baby's tummy.

"Okay, Sunshine," Jesse whispered to KC, "let's get you some clothes, and we'll go outside and let them sleep."

KC pushed up onto her bare feet and walked over to the pack that held the family's clothing. Opening the untied flap, she looked inside for something she could wear.

Jesse sat on the tent floor to pull her boots on. One advantage of going to bed in the condition Jennifer and she had the night before was that she was still partially dressed. She'd wait until her wife woke up before changing into fresh clothes.

KC walked over, her arms full of a shirt, a pair of britches, and underclothes. "Good girl," Jesse said as she took the items from her daughter and then helped KC pull off her sleeping shirt. Mother and daughter worked together to get KC dressed. "Where are your moccasins?" The soft yet resilient doeskin foot coverings had been given to KC by their friend Walks on the Wind.

"Ovuh dewe." KC pointed across the tent. "I git dem."

Jesse stood up while her daughter retrieved the moccasins. She snatched their coats off the top of one of the packs where they had been placed the day before and pulled hers on. Her shirt had been forgotten outside, and she was sure it would be a little chilly to put on after a night on the ground. Kneeling beside the packs, she carefully pulled out a circular object and stood. She turned and moved toward the tent opening and untied the door flap.

"Hewe, Mommy," KC whispered, holding up the moccasins. She still had a little trouble pulling the shoes on by herself.

"Hold on to them for a minute." Jesse scooped her daughter up into her arms and carried her outside. She dropped the tent flap down into place to keep the morning chill away from her sleeping wife and son. Turning, she looked for someplace to sit KC down while she put on her moccasins. Seeing nothing promising, as almost everything bore a covering of light morning dew, she settled for sitting cross-legged on the ground and placing KC in her lap. She quickly pulled on the girl's moccasins, then stood KC on her feet. "Here, let's get your coat on, then how about we get the fire going?" she asked as she helped KC push her arms into the coat sleeves.

KC frowned as Jesse buttoned up her coat. "It too hot, Mommy." The weather had been so dry and hot that most days she'd worn little more than a long shirt.

"It'll be hot soon enough, but until the sun comes up over the mountains it's a little too cold for you," Jesse explained as she stood up. She brushed at the dampness on the seat of her britches. "You keep it on until the chill leaves the air. We don't want you catching cold, do we?"

"Okay," KC agreed reluctantly.

With her daughter dressed, Jesse set to work getting the fire restarted and gathering more firewood. KC worked alongside her mother. When Jesse returned to camp with an armful of branches and deadfall, KC carried an armful of smaller twigs. Both piles were dropped next to the ring of stones around the fire. Jesse pulled one of the larger branches from her pile, laying it across the center of the ring, then set smaller branches against it. KC bent down, pulling a couple of long twigs from her pile and tossing them into the ring.

"Those should burn down into a nice bed of coals for cooking," Jesse said as she retrieved the odd object she had carried out of the tent earlier.

"What dat, Mommy?"

"A fish net. Should we see if we can catch a fish in it?"

"Yep." KC reached her hand up, smiling when her mother's much larger hand clasped it firmly. She half walked, half skipped beside Jesse toward the creek less than fifty feet from their campsite.

Over the years, the swiftly moving water had carved a deep channel in the soft earth, and the creek was bordered by vertical walls of dried mud that were deeper than Jesse was tall. Depending on the time of year, the water would fill the entire channel from one side to the other. Or, in periods of low water, like now, it would meander between its banks, exposing sections of its sandy bed.

When they reached the top of the creek bank, Jesse squatted to check out the possible locations for finding fish. She grinned when KC squatted beside her. "Couple of nice deep pools down there," she told her daughter. "Shouldn't be much trouble finding a fish or two."

"Dewe's one," KC whispered excitedly, pointing at a good sized trout swimming lazily in the crystal clear water.

"That's a nice one," Jesse agreed.

"You catch," KC told her momma, as if the outcome were already determined.

"I'll give it a try." Jesse smiled at her daughter's faith in her. "You stay put."

KC sat on the ground, wiggling around until her legs hung over the side of the steep drop-off. The heels of her moccasins bounced against the muddy soil as she watched her mother drop off the top of the bank and land in a small patch of wet sand below.

Being careful to position her body so her shadow wouldn't fall across the creek's surface, Jesse stepped into the creek, trying not to make any more of a disturbance than necessary. She eased away from the shore until the water was halfway up her boots, then bent over the fish net under the water.

The net was made from a sewing hoop she had seen one day in the dress shop Ruthie operated for them. Carefully secured to the hoop and floating behind it were a couple of feet of a very fine lace-like material she'd also taken from the shop's inventory. All that a fish had to do was swim through the hoop and into the net. Simple, or so Jesse hoped. This was the first time she had tested her creation.

The trout she and KC had seen came back into view, swimming right for the hoop. Jesse held her breath as the fish came nearer. As soon as its nose passed inside the ring, she swooped the hoop over its body. Pulling the net free of the water, Jesse struggled to keep control of the trout thrashing about inside. Not wanting to take any chances of losing her catch, she tossed the net, fish and all, up over her head in the direction of the bank.

KC saw the fish flying toward her. "Momma," she screamed, falling over backward to avoid being smacked in the face with the squiggling fish.

Turning at her daughter's scream, Jesse saw KC tumbling back away from the bank and out of sight. Afraid she had hit the girl with the fish, she scrambled upwards. Her fingers clawed at any possible hold while her boots slipped on the mud, but she managed to scale the slope and hurried to check on her daughter. She couldn't help but laugh when she spotted KC, uninjured but quite occupied.

Giggling hysterically, KC was rolling around on the ground with her little arms wrapped tightly around the trout still trapped inside the net. As the fish, almost as long as she was tall, flopped about uncontrollably, KC could do nothing but hang on.

Jennifer walked out of the tent with Charley. She was not at all happy at being awakened from a very enjoyable dream, but her stern look quickly melted at the sight of her daughter and wife. "I don't suppose I want to ask what you two are up to," she said as she approached the pair.

"Mommy catch fish," KC squealed as she was tossed about by their breakfast.

Jennifer laughed. "It looks to me like the fish has caught you, sweetie. See, Charley," she told the baby in her arms. "I told you they'd be up to trouble."

"Morning, darlin'," Jesse said as she bent down to take the fish away from KC. She carried it to a bucket of water by the fire where she dropped it, and the net that held it, into the water with a loud plop. She then turned toward Jennifer, arms extended and intending to wrap them around her wife.

Jennifer held out a warning hand. "Don't you come any closer."

"Huh?" Jesse stopped dead in her tracks. "What did I do?"

"It's not what you've done..." Jennifer giggled. "It's what you're trying to do."

"And what would that be?" Jesse started forward again, now that she knew Jennifer wasn't mad at her.

"Jesse Branson, I'm warning you — do not even think about hugging me."

Jesse stopped again. "Why not?"

KC giggled. "Mommy, you diw-ty."

"Huh?"

Charley pointed at Jesse, scrunching up his nose. "Bleck."

"What do ya mean?" Jesse dropped her head to look down the front of her. "Oh." She smirked at her mud-smeared clothing. She held up her hands up to inspect them and realized they were also covered in mud. She could only imagine what the rest of her looked like. "You mean you won't hug me like this?" Jesse asked, poking her lower lip out in a mock pout that mimicked her daughter's.

Jennifer growled. "If you have any plans for hugging me, you get right back in that creek and get washed off. And take KC with you."

Jesse looked down at her daughter, who also wore a thick layer of muck after rolling around on the ground with the slippery trout. "But, darlin'," Jesse protested, "that creek is a mite cold this morning."

Jennifer bit her lower lip in an attempt not to laugh at the pitiful look on her wife's face. "It wasn't too cold for you to go fishing."

"That's different. I was only standing in it."

"Go on." Jennifer pointed toward the creek. "I'll bring you some towels and clean clothes, and you can wash the ones you've got on."

"Come on, Sunshine. Seems we're needing a bath."

KC stood up. Before Jesse could grab her, the girl was racing for the edge of the creek bank.

Jesse and Jennifer watched in shock as KC leapt into the air. A moment later they heard a loud splash, followed by their daughter's high-pitched giggling.

Jennifer sighed. "Seems the creek isn't as cold as you think."

"Seems not."

"Well, don't just stand there, go see to our daughter. And tell her not to do that again. She about scared the life out of me."

Jesse shook her head in frustration and amusement as she followed her daughter. Standing on the edge of the drop-off, she looked down to see her daughter sitting in the creek and doing her best to pull off her dirty clothes. "KC Branson," Jesse scowled, hopping on one foot while she pulled the boot off the other, "you have got to stop," she switched feet to pull her other boot off, "doing that." Then, with a quick look over her shoulder in Jennifer's direction, she leapt into the air to join their daughter.

Jennifer watched Jesse disappear beneath the creek bank and listened to the squeals of delight coming from below. She hugged Charley. "It's a dang good thing you don't take after those two. Let's go get our young 'uns some dry clothes," she told the baby.

"Bleck."

Jesse guided Dusty along the leaf- and pine needle-covered ground. There was no trail to follow as she led her family over the mountains using a rarely traveled pass. It was a route she knew only because she had explored the canyon shortly after arriving in Sweetwater. At that time, she was still trying to decide whether she wanted to stay in the small town or sell the Silver Slipper and go back to a life drifting around the frontier. As she swayed easily with the movements of the horse, she remembered back to that day and how at peace she had felt riding through the thick forest accompanied only by the calls of the forest animals and the sound of water tumbling over rocks nearby. That sense of peace was the reason she had remained in Sweetwater. It made her feel that something good was going to happen to her if she stayed. Twisting around in the saddle to look at the woman riding behind her, she knew exactly what that had been.

"How are you doing, darlin'?" Jesse asked, smiling at the woman she loved.

Jennifer smiled back. "I'm fine, but I wouldn't say no to a break."

"There's a pretty spot not too far ahead," Jesse told her wife. "I figured we'd stop there for the night."

"All right. Charley is probably ready to get out of this carry sack for the day. How's KC?"

"Asleep." Jesse had her arm wrapped securely around the sleeping girl.

"I thought so." Jennifer grinned. "It's been way too quiet for the last hour."

"Yep." Jesse twisted back around in the saddle. Her eyes scanned the terrain in front of them as she looked for the clearing she remembered being alongside the creek they were following. Less than a half mile later, Jesse spotted the gap in the trees she had been watching for. She turned Dusty toward it, letting the big horse pick her own path over the rocky ground and around large boulders that had, hundreds of years before, tumbled down the steep slope on the opposite side of the creek.

The clearing was relatively flat compared to the stony, uneven ground they had been traveling. It was big enough for the tent to be set up and to have some open space around it before the trees closed back in. On the side facing the creek, a gentle slope dropped down a few feet to another level area much smaller than the clearing. A second drop-off ended right beside the creek. Unlike the clearing, the creek bed was angled, matching the tilt of the surrounding ground, its water rushing downward, plummeting over and around the boulders and fallen trees that littered its course.

Jesse swung out of the saddle, cradling KC as she dropped to the ground, then walked back to Blaze to help Jennifer to the ground with her free arm.

"It's a beautiful spot, sweetheart," Jennifer said, pulling her cane out of the scabbard she used to carry it. Leaning heavily on the cane, she explored the clearing, both to check out the campsite and to stretch out her tired muscles.

"We'll have to keep the young 'uns away from the creek," Jesse said. "Water's too swift here."

Jennifer walked toward the rapidly flowing water. "Yes, I do not want KC anywhere near that," she said when she returned to where Jesse was standing beside Boy.

"Here, darlin'." Jesse handed Jennifer her camp stool. It was the last thing she tied to the packs on Boy's back so that it could be the first to be removed whenever they stopped. "Sit for a bit."

"Actually, it feels better to be up and stretching it." Jennifer smiled, acknowledging her wife's thoughtfulness. "But maybe we can spread out a blanket for the children."

"Good idea." Jesse grunted. "What have you been feeding this one? She weighs more than Dusty."

Dusty whinnied, shaking her neck a few times, then reaching back to nibble at the saddle blanket on her back.

"I get the hint," Jesse growled at the horse. She shifted the sleeping girl in her arms to a more comfortable position. "Let me get the little ones taken care of, then I'll get your saddle off. They're a little more important than you are right now." Dusty swung her tail around, slapping Jesse in the back of the head.

Jennifer giggled. "Sweetheart, let me hold KC while you get the blanket. That way you can take care of Dusty before she whaps you again."

"Too many folk giving orders in this family," Jesse grumbled, handing the sleeping girl to her wife as Dusty snorted behind her.

"Mommy?" KC was climbing up Jesse's back.

"What, Sunshine?" Jesse asked. She was kneeling over Charley, changing his diaper.

"Go swim?"

"Not tonight, Sunshine. The water is too fast here."

"Humpft," KC grunted, pulling herself up using fistfuls of Jesse's shirt until she could hang her head over her mother's shoulder. "Hi, Cha-wie." Charley giggled when his sister popped into view. "You catch fish?" KC asked, making faces at her brother.

"Don't think we'd find many in that creek. Stop teasing your brother, or I'll never get his britches changed."

"Okay." KC let loose of Jesse's shirt and slid down her back. "Wheyuh Momma?"

"Good question." Jesse looked around the camp but saw no sign of her wife. "Darlin'?" she called out.

"I'm here, sweetheart."

Jesse looked in the direction from which Jennifer's reply had come, but she didn't see her wife. "Where here?"

"Back in the trees about twenty paces."

"What are you doing back there?"

"Jesse!"

"Oh." Jesse smirked, quickly deducing what her wife must be doing. "Sorry, darlin'. You okay? You've been gone a while."

"Yes, I'm fine. But can you come take a look at something?"

"Sure, just let me finish with Charley's britches." Jesse quickly completed the task of changing the baby's diaper. Walking to a pan of water, she set the dirty diaper aside to be washed out later, then used the soap bar put out earlier and scrubbed her hands. "Let's go find Momma," she told KC moments later as she lifted Charley off the blanket. KC held her hands in the air. Jesse grabbed the girl's hands, lifting her up into her free arm. "Give a holler, darlin', so I can find you."

"I'm here. Back the way we rode in, at that big boulder we passed."

"What are you doing all the way back there?" Jesse asked, making her way through the trees to find her wife.

"I saw something, and I was hoping I could see it better from here."

"Jennifer?" Jesse found the boulder but not her wife.

"Up here."

Jesse looked up. Standing several feet above her head was Jennifer. "How'd you get up there?"

"Walk around to the back, there's a dirt mound."

Jesse followed the directions. She hadn't paid much notice to the boulder when they rode past it earlier. About ten paces long and half that wide and tall, the boulder's size was impressive. The end of the mammoth rock was partially buried by a mountain of dirt worn smooth over the years by the forces of rain and wind. It wasn't a difficult walk up the side of the mound for Jesse, but she wondered how Jennifer had managed it with her cane.

"What are you doing all the way up here, darlin'?" Jesse asked when she reached the top of the mound and walked out onto the boulder.

"What do you think that is?" Jennifer pointed over the top of the forest. "I caught a glimpse of it through the trees from below and thought it looked strange."

Jesse looked to the north where far in the distance a portion of the sky appeared to be glowing red. She turned to look for the position of the sun. Although it was starting to set, she didn't think it could be causing the odd glow. "Don't rightly know, darlin'," she said. "Could just be a trick of the eye. This time of day, with the sun starting to drop, things look different."

"I know, but there's something about that." Jennifer shuddered. "It makes me feel…"

"What?"

"I'm not sure. But it's almost like it's a warning or something."

Jesse looked again at the strange glow. "Well, it could be…"

"What?"

"Nothing. Just letting my imagination get the better of me. It's probably just the setting sun. Whatever it is, it's a good distance away," Jesse said to reassure her wife. "We'll keep an eye on it as we ride, but I don't think it can do us any harm."

"You sure? It doesn't look like any sunset I've ever seen."

Jesse's stomach began to knot with a sense of foreboding. It was the same feeling she'd had when her father had tried to get her to move the cattle to higher ground. "We should be fine. Let's get off this rock before it gets too dark," she told Jennifer. "Don't know how you got up here in the first place. Good thing you didn't fall."

Jennifer bristled at the comment. "I'm not helpless, Jesse." Her leg limited her in many ways, but she refused not to do some things just because someone thought she shouldn't.

"Hey." Jesse softened her tone. With her arms full of babies, she could not do much more than stand and look at her upset wife. "I know you're not helpless. I've never said—

Jennifer placed her fingers against Jesse's lips. "I'm sorry," she whispered, leaning against the stronger woman. "I know you've never said anything like that."

"Or thought it," Jesse added as she leaned close to kiss Jennifer's brow.

"I know." Jennifer looked up, smiling warily at her wife.

"You okay?"

"Yes. It's just that ever since I saw that..." Jennifer's eyes turned toward the strange glow, "I've been a little edgy. Forgive me?"

"Nope." Jesse grinned. "Nothing to forgive. Now, let's get off this rock while we can still see."

CHAPTER NINE

Shortly before dawn, Jesse woke to the sound of the sides of the tent being buffeted by a strong wind. While waiting for her eyes to adjust to the lack of light, she felt Jennifer stirring beside her.

"What's wrong?" Jennifer asked sleepily as she snuggled closer. A moment later, she jerked upright when a loud crack exploded almost directly over their heads followed by something heavy brushing down the side of the tent. "Jesse?"

"Stay here." Jesse hugged Jennifer before releasing her to slip out of their bedroll. "Sounds like the wind came up during the night; it's probably just a branch breaking."

Straining to see Jesse as she moved away, Jennifer wrapped their blanket around her, her skin cooling once her wife left her alone in their bedroll. "There was hardly any breeze when we went to bed."

Jesse untied the tent flap, only to have it almost ripped out of her hand by the wind. "It's blowing now, darlin'," she said, sticking her head outside. Her face was assaulted by blowing twigs and leaves, and she ducked back into the relative safety of the tent. Retying the flap, she sniffed the air.

"Jesse, did the wind stir up our fire? I smell smoke," Jennifer whispered.

Jesse felt her way back to their bedroll, then bent down to retrieve her clothes. "I'm going out to check on the horses."

"Is that safe? It sounds like it's blowing pretty hard out there."

Jesse sat beside Jennifer to pull on her boots. "It is. But I need to go make sure they're all right. You best be getting dressed, too."

Jennifer reached out in the dark and found her wife's arm "Jesse, what aren't you telling me?"

Turning toward Jennifer, Jesse strained to see her wife's dim outline in the deep shadows inside the tent. "That glow in the sky last night..."

"What about it?"

"If it's what I think it was — and that smoke is a good indication that it is — then we may have to move and fast. I don't know why I didn't trust my instincts last night."

"What do you think it is?"

"Forest fire," Jesse said calmly, even though her insides were churning. If the forest was on fire, she was going to have to find a way to get her family someplace safe, and right now they were a long way in any direction from safety.

"Fire! Are we in danger?"

Jesse took Jennifer's hands into her own, holding them tight. "I don't think so, darlin', but it's hard to know," she answered honestly. "If that was a fire, I doubt it's come this far overnight. But fire makes it own wind that pulls it along. And as hard as it's blowing out there, it could pull a fire a long way. You best get dressed and get the young 'uns dressed. We'll decide what we're gonna do when I get back. Okay?"

"Okay."

"Let me get the lantern. You'll need to light it after I go out, otherwise the wind will blow it out for sure."

"You go; I'll get the lantern." Jennifer had a good idea where things were located in the tent, so she didn't think she'd have much trouble maneuvering about in the dark to locate the lantern and matches.

"Stay in the tent, please. I don't want to have to be worrying about you, too."

"I will."

Jesse leaned forward, placing a quick kiss on her wife's lips. "I won't be long."

"Be careful."

"I promise." Jesse found her coat and pulled it on, hoping it would provide some protection against the debris blowing about outside.

By the time Jesse stepped outside, Jennifer had already pulled on her denim pants. "I've got the lantern," she called as Jesse struggled to re-tie the tent flap. "Go on, I'll take care of this."

"Thanks, darlin'." The wind swirled around Jesse as she turned away from the tent. She could see little in the pre-dawn light as she made her way through the darkness to where she had picketed Blaze and Boy. "Dusty," she called out to the horse allowed to run free at night. She knew the palomino would not be too far from the campsite. She pulled her coat tight around her shoulders, holding the collar up to help protect her face. "Come on back, girl."

As she dressed, Jennifer could barely hear Jesse's calls and whistles above the wind. Tugging on her boots, she was comforted to hear Dusty trot past the side of the tent.

Jesse rubbed the mare's neck in greeting and was rewarded with a friendly nuzzling of her head. "Looks like we're in for a tryin' day. Do you smell it, girl?" Dusty whinnied, shaking her head as if to force the scent of danger from her nostrils. "I agree with you there." Jesse wiped at her own nose, the smoke more noticeable outside than it had been inside the tent. "Stick close to camp. It's going to be rough getting stuff packed up, I don't want to have to chase you down."

"Jesse?" Jennifer stood at the tent flap. She could hear the horses' nervous whinnies, but she was no longer able to discern her wife's movements.

Her mother's shout awakened her, and KC sat up and rubbed her eyes. "Momma?" she whimpered.

Jennifer knelt beside the children's bedroll. "It's okay, sweetie."

"It dawk," KC told her mother, unaccustomed to being awakened so early.

"I know, sweetie. But Mommy thinks we need to leave early today. So I need your help to get you and Charley dressed. Can you do that?"

"Cha-wie seep. He no wike dawk."

"He'll be fine. He has his big sister to help him. Can you pull off your nightshirt?"

"Yep."

With her daughter helping, Jennifer got KC dressed, then moved over beside the sleeping baby. Just as she lifted Charley into her arms, the tent flap opened and Jesse was swept inside by a gust of wind that blew out the lantern.

"Where'd you go?" Jennifer asked, reaching for the box of matches.

"To see if I could see anything from atop that boulder of yours," Jesse explained. "Matches?"

"Right here." Jennifer held the box out for Jesse and felt it taken from her hand. "And?"

"Couldn't see much more than what we saw last night. How are you doing in here?" Jesse asked as she relit the lantern and could see Jennifer kneeling beside the bedrolls, rocking the whimpering baby.

"KC is dressed. I was just getting Charley up."

"Is he all right?"

"Cha-wie no wike dawk," KC explained again to her mothers. The lantern's light wasn't strong enough to reach the darker corners of the tent.

"I'll start packing thinks up." Jesse reached down to ruffle KC's hair. "Sun's coming up. Soon as I get the packs on Boy, we'll leave."

"What about breakfast?" Jennifer asked. "The children should have something."

"Feed them what you can. Later we'll stop to feed them right."

"Are we going home?"

"No." Jesse was rolling up the empty bedrolls. "It's closer to continue on into to Philipsburg. If we push it, we can be there tonight."

"What if it's moving that way?" Jennifer asked, careful not to say "fire" in front of her daughter, who had finally stopped being afraid after experiencing being trapped inside the burning Slipper.

"Even if it is, it's safer to be there than in the trees. And we'd be in woods and brush almost all the way back to the ranch. If we keep going, we should be clear of the forest by midday and into open valleys. We can stick close to the rivers and creeks then."

Jennifer wasn't as convinced as Jesse that going back was a bad idea, but she was still learning about living on the frontier, and she put her trust in her wife to keep their family safe. Charley was changed and dressed, and when Jennifer tried to stand, she found her leg had cramped from being bent for so long. "KC, come sit with your brother while I help Mommy. Sweetheart, can you help me up?"

"Sure, darlin'."

"Do you know where my cane is?" Jesse bent to retrieve the cane from the tent floor and handed it to her wife. "Thanks. What do you want me to do?"

"Get them fed and put what you can into the packs. I'll take care of the rest and get the packs tied up as soon as I get Dusty and Blaze saddled."

KC walked to Jesse and tugged on her pant leg. "Mommy," she said, looking up at her mother with worry on her face.

Jesse knelt down to talk to her daughter. "What's wrong, Sunshine?"

"Smoke, Mommy. I smews it."

"I know. I think there's a big fire in the forest, but it's a long way away from us. The wind is carrying the smoke and making it smell bad." Jesse pulled the girl to her. "It's not like before, Sunshine, not like when you and Charley were in the Slipper." She hugged KC. "We're fine. But just to be sure, we're going to get packed up and ride on to Philipsburg. Momma is going to need your help watching Charley."

"I watch him good, Mommy. He not hide ag'in."

Jesse kissed KC on the forehead. "That's my girl. You help Momma while I get the horses ready."

"Okay."

The wind had steadily increased since they'd left camp early in the morning. Debris picked up from the forest floor or knocked loose from the trees was being blown about. The smoke had also thickened, irritating noses and eyes but not yet a serious threat to breathing.

Jesse looked back over her shoulder, making sure Jennifer was staying close as the horses cantered across a small meadow. She would have liked to push them faster but didn't want to strain their burdened pack horse trailing Dusty on a long lead. They had been riding non-stop for a couple of hours, and she knew she needed to find a place to rest the horses and her family. With the tall trees blocking their view, they had only the wind and smoke to assess any danger they might be riding toward. And being in the middle of a grassy meadow surrounded by forest was not the place to stop. She would have to keep looking.

KC tilted her head back to look up at her mother. "Mommy, I ti-wed," she said, rubbing her stinging eyes.

"I know, Sunshine." Jesse rubbed her daughter's tummy soothingly. "We'll stop just as soon as we get out of the forest. Okay?"

KC sighed. "Okay." She squirmed about until she could rest her head against the arm wrapped around her.

Jesse took another quick glance over her shoulder. She was glad they had the carry sack for Charley so Jennifer didn't have the added worry of having to hold the baby and hold on to Blaze's reins. Facing forward again, Jesse concentrated on her surroundings. If her memory of the area was accurate, they should have only a few miles to go before they would leave the forest behind them. They would still have some potential problem areas after that, but they would have the benefit of being on open ground and, hopefully, able to see what direction the fire was moving. As the meadow ended and they rode back into the trees, she slowed Dusty to a trot; it would do no good for any of the horses to injure a leg on the rougher ground under the trees.

"Jesse," Jennifer called out as soon as Blaze slowed and she could relax her grip on the saddle, "how much further until we can rest?" Her leg was throbbing, and she desperately needed to stretch her cramping muscles.

"Not sure, darlin'," Jesse called back. "May have to wait until we clear this last stretch of trees."

"How long?"

"Hour, maybe more."

"I can't, Jesse." Jennifer grimaced as a spasm sent explosions through her leg. She shifted in the saddle in an attempt to relieve the pain. "I have to stop."

Hearing the anguish in her wife's voice, Jesse slowed Dusty to a walk. Her eyes scanned the area seeking any place that would provide a safe haven, if only for a few minutes. She heard water tumbling over rocks and nudged Dusty in the direction of the source. "Come on," she told Jennifer. "We'll find a place by the water." Without comment, Jennifer turned Blaze to follow.

After a hundred feet, Dusty walked between a pair of trees, stopping abruptly as the ground dropped off sharply at her feet. "Back up, girl," Jesse encouraged.

"What's wrong?" Jennifer asked, unable to see past the larger horse and her wife.

"Need to find a better spot to get to the creek," Jesse explained as she guided Dusty around a tangled thicket of underbrush. "Come this way. It's better," she told Jennifer. The mare eased down a gentler slope, then walked out onto an exposed gravel bar, the creek flowing around the far edge of the pebble-covered ground. The gravel bar allowed just enough room for the horses to stand and drink without having to step into the fast-moving water. Tightening her hold on KC, Jesse swung her leg over the saddle horn and slipped down to the ground. "Stay put," she told the girl as she stood her on the ground, "while I help Momma."

"Okay." KC stood where her mommy had placed her, twisting to look around behind her.

Jesse walked around Blaze, then took hold of Jennifer's waist and helped her down from the saddle. The grimace on her wife's face told her all she needed to know about how she was feeling. With Jennifer leaning heavily against her, she pulled the cane free of the scabbard and handed it to her wife. "Do you want to stand or lay down, darlin'?"

Jennifer reached down, kneading her fingers into the aching tissue as she attempted to ease the piercing pain. "I need the muscles rubbed, Jesse."

Deciding the gravel bar would not be comfortable for Jennifer, Jesse led her back a few feet to the moss-covered creek bank and eased her down to sitting.

"Let me get Charley off you," Jesse said, holding the carry sack so Jennifer could pull her arms free. "Come over here, Sunshine," she called to KC, who was occupying herself by picking up handfuls of the pea-sized gravel and tossing it into the rushing waters. KC bent down to fill her hands again before following her mommy's instructions. "Here you go, Charley." Jesse smiled at the baby, pulling him free of the carry sack. "You sit right here for a bit. KC will come sit with you." With the children taken care of for the moment, Jesse turned her attention back to Jennifer. "Lay back and I'll rub that leg for you."

"Let me roll over," Jennifer said as she eased herself onto her belly. Before she even had the time to lie flat, Jesse was working on her cramped muscles.

KC managed to walk across the gravel bar and up the slope of the bank without dropping any of her treasures. Plopping down beside her brother, she opened her hands. "'Ook, Cha-wie. Baby wocks, just wike you." Charley reached out, picking a single pebble out of his sister's hands, then pulled his hand back, intending to put the tiny stone in his mouth. "No, Cha-wie." KC laughed. "You can't eat it." Dropping the pebbles in front of her, she retrieved the one from her brother. "Dey wocks. Ya t'wow dem." She demonstrated for the baby, giggling when the pebble bounced off a nearby tree.

Charley smiled, reaching again for the pile of pebbles and picking one off the top. He pulled his hand back, then let the pebble fly. It hit the ground just inches from where he sat.

KC frowned at her brother's performance. "You too wittuh to t'wow wocks," she grumbled. "You gots to gwow."

Jennifer listened to the exchange between her children, glad KC didn't seem as concerned with the smoke-filled air.

"Feelin' better, darlin'," Jesse asked, still massaging the stiff leg.

Jennifer sighed. "Much. You just keep doing whatever it is you're doing, and I'll be ready to ride in no time."

"Good." Jesse looked skyward. The smoke was getting thicker, and she figured that couldn't be a good sign.

"Ack." KC coughed. "Mommy, huwts." She rubbed her eyes, and Charley did the same.

"I know, Sunshine," Jesse told her daughter.

"Is there something we can do for them?"

"Keep their faces wet down is the best I can think of," Jesse said. "Ain't much else we can do about the smoke."

Jennifer rolled over and held her hands out to Jesse. "Help me up."

"Are you sure?" Jesse was surprised that Jennifer would be ready to get up so soon.

"Jesse, let's wash their faces and get them something to eat. I want to get moving and get them out of this smoke as soon as possible."

"You sure?" Jesse asked again, not wanting Jennifer to feel they had to move right away but glad that she seemed ready to.

"Yes, now help me up, sweetheart."

"All right." Jesse stood, then pulled Jennifer to her feet. "What do we have for them?"

"We still have a couple of biscuits left from last night and some cheese. That'll have to do for now. Can you get that out and a clean cloth to wash their faces?"

"Be right back."

"Stay put," KC told Charley as she pushed herself to her feet to follow Jesse back to the horses.

Jennifer grinned; her daughter was so much like Jesse. "Come on, little man," she said, bending down to pick up the baby. Her leg protested, but she forced back the pain, refusing to let her leg put her family in further danger. "Uh, oh." She wrinkled her nose. "Somebody needs some fresh britches."

"I'll take care of him," Jesse said, pulling a clean towel out of a pack. "Take this to Momma," she said, giving the cloth to KC standing beside her.

"Okay."

"Sweetheart, can you soak it in the creek first?"

"Yep." Jesse leaned down and wrapped an arm around KC's waist, then carried her to the edge of the creek and held her over the water, lowering her giggling daughter until she was able to dunk the towel under the surface of the water. "Okay, take that to Momma. And try not to get too wet." She set KC down, sending her on her way with a playful swat on the bottom.

Finally, Jennifer thought when Blaze carried her out of the forest into a long narrow valley with a creek flowing down its center. Riding up alongside where Dusty stood, she pulled Blaze to a stop.

Jesse was looking to the north and not at all liking what she was seeing. Thick, black smoke billowed high into the sky over a series of hills several miles away.

"Jesse?" Jennifer whispered, alarmed by the frightening sight.

"I know." Jesse reached out and placed her hand around her wife's. "Looks like the wind is blowing the fire to the west."

"Toward the ranch? And Sweetwater?"

Jesse's heart sank as she admitted to herself that it was a possibility. "Can't worry about that now," she said, hoping the fire would burn out before it got that far.

"What do you think started it?" Jennifer asked, unable to take her eyes off the menacing clouds of churning smoke.

"Lightning, most likely. Gets dry like it has and we get plenty of dry lightning storms over the mountains. Come on, let's get moving."

Jennifer turned away from the smoke clouds only when Blaze moved to follow Dusty. She was glad they were no longer riding among trees, but she wondered how safe it was for them to be riding through a valley of dried grasses and bushes. "How far away do you think the fire is?"

"Thirty, forty miles," Jesse said.

"How far to Philipsburg?"

"'Bout ten."

"How fast can the fire move?"

"Fast as it wants." Jesse nudged Dusty to increase her speed.

CHAPTER TEN

Leaving the forest, the women followed a creek as it snaked along the floor of a narrow valley. They reached the end of the valley where the small creek merged into a larger one flowing north through a much wider but shorter valley. A wagon road, not much more than two parallel ruts worn into the hard ground, paralleled the new creek before disappearing over a rise to the south. Jennifer became alarmed when Jesse turned to follow the wagon road northward. The new direction would take them directly toward the smoke clouds.

"Are you sure we should be riding toward the fire?"

"Ain't got much choice, darlin'," Jesse explained. "We need to get around this stretch of bluffs to get to the pass to Philipsburg."

"Can't we keep riding east? There must be a trail over the top."

"Might be, but those bluffs are steep and we don't have time to look for one. We've got a long climb coming, and it'll be hard enough on the horses without tiring them out on a goose chase." Jesse pulled Dusty to a stop where the bank sloped gently down to the creek. "Good spot to rest for a bit."

Fretful, Jennifer looked into the distance ahead of them. The sky was black with thick clouds of smoke and, even though they looked to be some distance away, she was sure that every now and then she could see bursts of flame exploding below them. Apprehensive, she guided Blaze down to the creek.

Jesse was already out of the saddle when Jennifer rode up. Setting KC down a short distance from where the horses were drinking, she walked back to help Jennifer to the ground. Jennifer smiled as Jesse handed up her cane while checking on Charley, the carry sack having been switched to the front so she could calm the agitated baby. "How's he doing?" Jesse asked.

"Better since he can see me now. He needs changing."

"I'll get a diaper. What do we have to feed them?"

"Not much, just the last of the cheese and bread." Jennifer and Jesse had gone without food all day so they could save what they had for the children. Without stopping long enough to build a cook fire, they were limited as to which of their supplies were readily edible. "What about going up the road in the other direction, Jesse? Is there a town that way?"

"Not that I know of, probably just goes back to some ranch." Jesse handed the last of the prepared food to Jennifer to dole out to KC and Charley.

"But wouldn't that be safer? At least we'd be riding away from the fire."

"Maybe, if it was the only fire." Jesse took the carry sack off Jennifer and sat on the ground, spreading her legs to lay Charley on top of the sack so she could change him. "I don't know that area, so if we got into trouble—"

"What do you mean *only* fire?" Jennifer asked, breaking off a morsel of cheese and giving it to KC.

"If it was lightning that caused that big one, there's a good chance there's other fires out there. That's why we need to get to Philipsburg."

"You could have told me this before now," Jennifer said, looking warily at the ridges of hills and bluffs flanking the valley.

"Didn't see a need to worry you more than you already are."

"Jesse…" Jennifer sat beside her wife, "you don't think I can handle it, do you?"

"It's not that. It's—"

"This is my family, too, and I will do what I need to protect it. I'm not a helpless little girl, Jesse."

Jesse sighed. She finished redressing Charley, then sat back and pulled him into her lap. "I'm just doing the best I know how, darlin'."

Jennifer broke off a piece of bread for the baby and held it out to him. He grabbed it hungrily. "I know." She leaned against her wife. "I'm scared, Jesse," she whispered.

"Me, too. But we'll get through this… Together."

"Together."

Jesse let out a sigh of relief when they reached the junction of their valley with two other valleys where they would cross the creek and start riding east again. Dusty stopped and lowered her head to take a welcome drink and Boy moved up to do the same. Jesse scanned the route on the other side of the creek. Almost as soon the wagon road crossed the creek, it turned to skirt around the base of a knoll. The grade steepened as the road began the long climb Jesse had warned of.

When Blaze dropped his head to the creek, Jennifer used the short rest to look ahead. Her eyes traced the road as it wound its way up the sides of hills, traveling steadily upward to the top of a ridge. "Where's Philipsburg?"

"Other side of the crest." Jesse pointed far above them. "We'll be able to see it as soon as we get up there."

"Mommy?" KC squirmed in the saddle.

"What, Sunshine?"

"Me ti-wed."

"I know," Jesse rubbed the girl's tummy. "But we can't stop until we get over the top."

It had been a long day, and they still had quite a distance to travel before it would end. KC started to whimper. She was tired, her eyes stung from the smoke in the air, and her bottom was sore from riding all day. Jesse took pity on her daughter, lifting her up to stand on the saddle. It wasn't much of a change, but it might help for a short time. "How's this?" she asked KC.

"Dis betteh." KC grinned, turning around to face Jesse. "You ho'd me, okay?"

"Sure will." Jesse watched as KC squirmed about, trying different positions. The girl finally ended up stretched across the saddle, her head resting on one of her mother's thighs while her feet hung over the other. "But if I need to sit you back up, you go," Jesse said, not knowing what might happen or when.

"Okay." KC giggled, glad to be able to move a little.

"Wind's picking up again," Jennifer commented as a draft of warm air blew past them.

Jesse looked around. Their situation was not favorable as they would soon be enclosed by the steep sides of the hills and unable to see very far in any direction. "Best we get to the top," she said, nudging Dusty into motion.

The women had ridden almost to the crest of the ridge and were thankful that the road wasn't quite as steep as they neared the top. The slopes on either side of them were also flattening out, and they were able to see beyond their immediate surroundings.

Jennifer brushed soot off Charley's face. The higher they climbed, the more soot and ash seemed to fall out of the sky, coating all of them and the horses in a layer of gray. She glanced upward, hoping to see the crest had been reached. Instead, she was shocked to see wisps of smoke coiling around the trees along the ridge. "Jesse, look!" she cried, pulling Blaze to a stop.

"Damn!" Jesse muttered, seeing what had alarmed her wife. She looked for someplace, any place, her family could seek shelter. The smoke-filled sky allowed little sunlight through, casting gray shadows over everything, and she almost missed the opening in the side of the hill. When she looked back to the top of the ridge, the smoke had thickened substantially and she knew whatever was the cause of it was moving fast. She nudged Dusty as close to Blaze as she could. "See that mine shaft about a third of the way up the hill?" she asked Jennifer, pointing to the opening.

"Yes."

"Take KC and get up there." Jesse passed the girl to her wife. "Cut Blaze loose and go inside the tunnel. Get as far back as you can."

"What about you?" Jennifer cried.

The wind was strengthening, and gusts of hot air boiled over the top of the ridge and down onto the riders.

"I'll be there in a minute. I have to do something first. Go, we don't have time to argue." As Jennifer rode for the mine shaft, Jesse tugged on Boy's lead, bringing the pack horse up beside Dusty. Reaching for the bedrolls tied to the top of the packs, she pulled them loose, then dropped the lead reins to Boy and turned Dusty around. The horse was soon galloping back down to the creek below.

Jesse leapt out of the saddle as soon as Dusty reached the bank. Running into the creek, she pushed the blankets under the current to soak up as much of the water as they could, then, carrying the sopping blankets, she swung up into the saddle. Dusty was galloping up the road before she had both boots in the stirrups.

Trying to protect KC and Charley from the burning debris falling around them, Jennifer slipped off of Blaze as soon as the horse stood beside the mine entrance. She set KC on the ground and then pulled her cane free. "Hold my hand," she told her daughter before leading her inside the dark tunnel and limping several strides down its length before stopping. Settling the children on the packed dirt, she turned and hurried back to the entrance to wait for Jesse.

Dusty raced back to the mine tunnel, her strong legs charging up the incline with little trouble. Jesse swung off the mare's back, pulling the wet blankets with her. Taking a final glance up to the top of the ridge, she found the trees fully engulfed in flames. "Get out of here, girl," she told Dusty, tossing the reins over the saddle. "Take the others and get someplace safe."

Dusty whinnied, then galloped down the ravine followed by Blaze and Boy, the three horses disappearing into the hills.

"You need to get back some," Jesse told Jennifer when she found her waiting at the mine's entrance. Grabbing her wife around the waist, she led her into the tunnel. When it became too dangerous to go any further, Jesse dropped the bedrolls on the ground. "Sit here," she told Jennifer and helped her down. KC clung to her leg, and she picked her up and placed her in Jennifer's lap. "Sit with Momma. And stay here, all of you." With no time to lose, Jesse lifted one of the wet bedrolls. "Stay under this; it'll help keep the smoke away from you. Keep the young 'uns safe," she told Jennifer as she dropped the blanket over the top of her wife and children.

"Jesse!" Jennifer screamed, realizing Jesse wasn't going to join them. "Where are you going?"

"To try and keep the smoke out of the tunnel!" Jesse yelled as she hurried back to the mine entrance carrying the other bedroll. Smoke was already curling around the tunnel's opening. Lifting the wet bedroll, she stretched it across the tunnel entrance, blocking the smoke's access. As the fire approached, the wind grew stronger and she had to struggle to hold onto the blanket, finally having to stand on the bottom of the blanket to keep it in place.

Outside of the tunnel, the side of the ravine was ablaze with fire that consumed everything in its path. Fed by the dried grass and brush, flames raced downhill in front of the wind it was helping create.

Despite Jesse's efforts, thick smoke seeped past the edges of the blanket and billowed into the mine shaft. As the smoke churned around her, she had trouble breathing, but she refused to give up. Stretching her arms and legs as wide as possible, she attempted to cover more of the opening. The heat of the fire had evaporated all the moisture from the blanket, and Jesse knew that at any minute the blanket itself could burst into flames. But she wasn't about to let go of it and give the smoke and fire free access to her family huddled behind her. She struggled to draw air into her protesting lungs, coughing violently when toxic smoke filled them instead, making her sick. As she desperately protected Jennifer and the babies, her legs buckled beneath her.

The freight wagon rumbled over the top of the rise, the driver working hard to control the team pulling it. With so much smoke and burning debris in the air, the horses were spooked and on the verge of becoming runaways at every step. As the wagon approached the junction of the three valleys, the driver could see the dark swath left behind by the recent flames. The horses slowed their steps, not anxious to cross the still-smoking ground.

The driver pulled back on the reins. "Whoa, ya nags, no sense going any further 'til I can see what's going on." Standing gave the driver a better view of the aftermath of the fire. It was apparent the flames had come over the top of the ridge, swept down the hills, and burned themselves out when they met up with the creek. "Lucky for us it must've been moving too fast to spread much," the driver told the team of horses, settling back on the bench seat. Reins snapping on their rumps encouraged the team to start moving again. "We've been lollygagging long enough. I said I'd be home by dark, and I don't aim to keep her waiting."

The team moved out slowly, pulling the heavy wagon behind it. As they started up the incline, the driver was surprised to see two saddled horses and a pack horse coming out of a gully and toward the creek.

"Wonder who those belong to. Whoa," the driver called to the team. "Best have me a look, case someone's hurt." Setting the wagon brake, the driver climbed down from the high seat. Boots kicking up small clouds of dust and soot in the blackened earth, the driver approached Blaze, holding out a hand to grab the reins. Dusty whinnied and Blaze moved back a few feet. The driver tried again, and Dusty again warned Blaze away. "If'n that's the way you plans to be, to heck with ya. I can't stick around here all day," the driver grumbled, returning to the wagon and waiting team. "Just hope whoever you belongs to ain't needin' help."

Jennifer could stay under the blanket no longer. She'd heard Jesse's coughing at first, but then for the past several minutes, no sounds had come from the end of the tunnel. She tentatively lifted the edge of the blanket and peeked out from underneath it. She could see the mine opening starkly outlined by the dark tunnel walls and a layer of smoke curling along the top of the shaft, but there was no sign of Jesse. Jennifer threw the blanket aside.

"Momma?" KC, glad to be free of the stifling blanket, searched for her mother in the darkness.

"I'm right here, sweetie," Jennifer reached out to reassure her daughter. "Are you okay?"

"Whewe Mommy?"

"I don't know, but we'll go look for her as soon as I can get up." Jennifer's leg was stiff from sitting on the cold ground for so long. She reached out with her hands, searching for her cane, grateful when her fingers wrapped around it. She struggled to her feet, standing for several moments to allow her body to become oriented to the new position.

KC moved closer to her mother, hugging her leg. "Give me your hand, sweetie." Jennifer reached down to take hold of the frightened girl's outstretched hand. "Let's go find Mommy."

Jennifer wasn't sure what she would find when she reached the end of the tunnel, but it couldn't be any worse than not knowing. She could tell the fire had moved past because there were no flames visible outside the opening and the smoke was not nearly as bad as it had been when she and the children were hunched under the blanket. She had almost reached the tunnel entrance when she spotted her wife's crumpled form. "Jesse!" she cried.

KC spied her mommy at the same time. Pulling free of Jennifer, she ran to Jesse's side. "Mommy!" KC cried, patting Jesse arm. "Mommy!"

Jennifer dropped to her knees beside Jesse and bent over, pressing an ear to her wife's chest. She heard a faint but steady heartbeat. "Thank goodness!" she exclaimed. Using her cane, she pushed herself up to standing, then carried Charley outside. "Come sit with Charley," she called to KC, who had remained with Jesse. When her daughter appeared, she returned inside the tunnel. Her cane, now more of a hindrance than a help, was tossed aside as she stood at Jesse's head. Bending over, she slipped her arms under her wife's and hefted her shoulders off the ground. It took several attempts, but she finally managed to drag Jesse out of the tunnel. She didn't take any time to rest before examining her wife for injuries. She was more than relieved when she discovered that, except for a few minor burns on her hands, Jesse was unscathed. But that didn't explain why she wasn't awake.

"Momma, ook."

Jennifer glanced at her daughter, who was pointing toward the road where a team of horses was slowly pulling a freight wagon up the incline. She started waving and calling to the driver. KC added her shouts to her mother's.

The driver, hearing the calls, looked up to see a woman kneeling on the ground just outside a mine entrance. She was waving her arms and shouting, as was a child jumping up and down beside her. "What the…"

"Hurry, please," Jennifer called down to the driver. The wagon was on a section of road a hundred feet below the mine entrance.

Not wanting to leave the team standing on the grade with the full weight of the wagon dragging on them, the driver guided the horses to a relatively flat piece of ground just off the road before climbing down from the seat.

"Do you have water? We need water," Jennifer called again.

Climbing back up to retrieve a canteen from under the seat, the driver also grabbed the kit of bandages and salves carried to treat any injuries the team of horses might suffer. It took several minutes to scramble up the side of the ravine to the woman and child.

"Thank you," Jennifer said, accepting the offered canteen. She allowed both KC and Charley a drink before sitting to lift Jesse's head into her lap.

"What happened?"

"The fire came over the ridge. Jesse got us inside." Jennifer dipped her fingers in the water and moistened Jesse's lips.

The driver looked around. "No wagon. No horses. How'd you git here?"

"We set our horses free."

"Must be the three I seen down at the creek. You've a long walk to try and catch them."

"We won't have to, they'll come back."

Remembering how the horses had shied away earlier, the driver said, "Doubt it."

"They'll come."

"What's wrong with him?" the driver asked.

"I'm not sure. I can't find any place she's hurt—"

"She?"

"Yes, Jesse is my..." Jennifer almost said wife but stopped herself. She and Jesse were careful not to reveal their true relationship when they traveled outside of Sweetwater. "Sister," she finished.

"Probably sucked in too much of the smoke."

"Is there something we can do for her?" Jennifer asked, concerned that Jesse was showing no signs of waking.

"Nothin' I know of. Where you from?"

"Sweetwater."

"You're a long way from home. What're you doin' out here?"

"We're going to Granite. We have a friend there."

"Granite, huh?"

"Yes."

"Mind me asking the name of your friend?"

"Leevie Temple. Do you know her?" The driver took off her hat to scratch her head, and Jennifer was startled to see long hair tumble free. "You're a woman." She looked at the freight wagon, then back at the driver. "Are you Dannie?"

"Leevie didn't say nothin' 'bout having visitors."

"She doesn't know we're coming. I, uh...I wanted to surprise her."

"You that schoolteacher she's always talking 'bout?"

Jennifer smiled. "I guess I probably am."

"Then that ain't your sister," Dannie nodded at Jesse, "is it?"

"No. Jesse is not my sister."

"Thought she was smarter'n that by the way Leevie talks about her."

"Smarter than what?" Jennifer's eyes narrowed as she waited for further explanation.

"Smarter than to bring her wife and young 'uns out like this. Damn fool thing to do."

Jennifer was about to give the disdainful woman a piece of her mind, when Jesse started coughing.

"Mommy, you diw-ty." KC sat at Jesse's side, holding a bandaged hand. The soot-covered rancher was still having trouble breathing and couldn't yet sit up.

"You look a mite dirty yourself," Jesse rasped, her throat irritated by the smoke she had inhaled.

Jennifer poured a swallow of water into her wife's mouth. She held Jesse's head in her lap. "You shouldn't try to talk, sweetheart."

Charley, sitting beside his momma, crawled to Jesse and started to climb up on top of her.

"Best you keep him off her," Dannie said. She was wrapping a bandage around Jesse's hand.

"Come here, Charley." Jennifer leaned forward to remove the baby.

Jesse coughed. "Leave him be."

"Are you sure, sweetheart? You're having trouble breathing as it is."

"Leave him."

Dannie shook her head. "Fool thing to do."

Jennifer glared at the woman. "I wish you'd stop referring to Jesse that way. She's not a fool."

"Momma." KC pointed down the ravine. "'Ook, Dusty coming. And Baze."

"Thank goodness." Jennifer sighed, glad to see the horses return without having to be chased down. "I wonder if Boy is with them."

"Boy?" Dannie asked.

"Our pack horse," Jennifer explained, watching the tired horses' slow progress up the ravine.

"Dewe Boy!" KC shouted excitedly when the big draft horse plodded into view.

Jennifer smiled: her family was back together. "And he still has the packs." After watching the horses gallop away from the fire, she'd been sure the packs would get shaken loose and fall off.

"Need to make sure they're all right," Jesse rasped, struggling to sit up.

"Stay put," KC scolded her mother. "Momma say so."

Jennifer smirked and pulled Jesse back down. "She's right, sweetheart. You need to rest. They look to be okay, but I'll check them over when they get here."

Dusty walked up to stand beside her prone mistress. She dropped her head, nuzzling Jesse's face. "You okay, girl?" Jesse wheezed, rubbing the mare's nose. For an answer, Dusty blew out a short blast of air, disturbing the layer of ash on the rancher.

KC broke into giggles, her arms waving futilely at the cloud of soot engulfing her and resettling on Jesse.

Charley sneezed. "Bleck." He scratched his nose.

"We best get moving." Jesse looked up at Jennifer. "Help me up so I can get mounted."

"That ain't too good an idea," Dannie said. She had stood and was checking the horses, which now made no attempt to avoid her.

"What do you mean?" Jennifer asked.

"If she tries to ride, she'll be falling off in no time. Lungs are still full of smoke; she needs to let them clean out."

"How long will that take?"

"Depends."

"On what?"

"On how much smoke she breathed in."

Jennifer studied Jesse. She could see her wife was struggling to draw in air with each breath she took. "I guess we'll have to camp here for a few days, sweetheart. At least we won't have to worry about a fire coming this way again."

Dannie scratched her head, unsure what to do. She could go about her business, leaving the women and their children to fend for themselves. "Best we load her into the back of the wagon," she told Jennifer. "It'll be a rough ride, but she won't be falling off no horse that way. Since ya was on your way to visit Leevie, I might as well make sure you get there."

Jennifer smiled. "Thank you." She tried to stand, then remembered her cane was still inside the tunnel. "Would you be kind enough to retrieve my cane? I can't walk without it."

"Where is it?"

"In dewe," KC said, pointing into the mine.

Dannie frowned but walked into the dark tunnel. She returned a few minutes later with the cane and their bedrolls. "One's a bit scorched, but there's some use left in it," she said as she gave the cane to Jennifer, then helped Jesse to her feet. "Best get you to the wagon."

With Jesse settled in the back of the wagon, Dannie lifted first KC, then Charley into the bed to sit with their mommy. "Let me get your horses tied to the wagon," she said, securing the removable gate at back of the wagon.

"You don't need to tie them," Jennifer said, wrapping Blaze's reins around the saddle horn making sure to leave plenty of slack in the rawhide for the horse to have free movement, then she stepped beside Dusty to do the same.

"Ain't you afraid they'll run away?"

"No." Jennifer rubbed Dusty's neck. "Dusty won't leave Jesse, and Blaze and Boy follow Dusty."

Dannie thought about arguing but after seeing the mare's behavior at the creek, she figured Jennifer must know what she was talking about. She looped Boy's lead around the packs to keep it from dragging on the ground. "Let's get you up in the seat and we'll go."

Jennifer let Dannie help her. The freight wagon was much bigger than the ranch buckboard, and she was grateful for the assistance. Her only regret was that it wasn't Jesse's hands on her waist as she used the spokes of the large wagon wheel to clamber up to the seat.

"Do you…" Jennifer hesitated when Dannie climbed up to sit beside her. She didn't want to ask more of the woman helping them, but she knew her children were hungry. "Would you happen to have any food? They've had so little all day."

"Don't have much but…" Dannie reached under the wagon seat and pulled out a basket and handed it to Jennifer. "You're welcome to what's here. Leevie always sends me off with a full basket." Wrapped in a cloth were the remains of a loaf of bread, some cheese, a couple of slices of ham, and pieces of an apple. "Sorry, I ate most of it."

"Thank you. It's very generous of you." Jennifer leaned over the back of the wagon seat. "KC, take this." She held the basket for her daughter. "Give Charley little bites."

KC took the basket and carried it back to where she'd been sitting beside Jesse. Plopping down, she placed the basket in her lap. She smiled as she uncovered the goodies it held. "'Ook, Cha-wie. Tweats. You eats dis." She pulled a hunk of bread free, handing it to her brother. "Mommy, you eats," she commanded, holding a piece of apple out to Jesse.

"Don't think I should," Jesse rasped, not sure she could get the piece of fruit down her raw throat. "But I'd like another drink of water."

"No tawks." KC frowned at her mother. "Momma says no tawks."

Jesse smiled, ruffling her daughter's hair. She lifted the canteen to her lips and let a little water flow into her mouth.

Dannie slapped the reins on her team's rumps and the horses strained against their harnesses, starting the wagon in motion. As she guided the team back onto the road, Dannie looked over her shoulder to see the three horses were indeed following behind.

CHAPTER ELEVEN

The heavy freight wagon crested the top of the ridge. The team of horses, just moments before straining to pull its load uphill, now struggled to keep the wagon from overtaking them as the grade shifted downward.

Spotting a cluster of buildings on the opposite side of the valley, Jennifer asked, "Is that Philipsburg?"

Dannie grunted, her leg pressing hard against the wagon's brake handle to help control their descent. "Yes."

"Where's Granite?"

"Top of the mountain behind it."

Jennifer sighed. She had hoped their journey would soon be ending, but by the looks of the distance they still had to cover, it would be long after nightfall before they reached the mining camp. Her eyes surveyed the hillside across which the road sliced on its way to the valley floor. The blackened path of the fire that had threatened them stood out clearly on the otherwise untouched terrain. The flames had begun in a coppice of trees far to the south, burning along the ridgeline before finally flowing over the crest to endanger her family.

At the sound of Jesse suffering through another bout of coughing, Jennifer twisted around in the seat. Seeing the drawn look on her wife's face and the tired children that were draped over her body, she told Dannie, "We need to stop."

"We'll be there in another couple of hours," Dannie said, not anxious to delay her homecoming any longer. She had left Granite before dawn the day before to make the delivery of supplies to a ranch several miles south and had promised Leevie she'd be home tonight. She'd already lost precious time when she'd stopped to help this family. She turned to look into the back of the wagon. Jesse's coughing had lessened, and she was relaxing again. "She'll be fine."

Jennifer frowned. Facing forward again, she searched for someplace they could stop and rest, maybe even camp for the night. A thicket of trees beside the road at the base of the hill caught her eye. "Is there water there?" she asked, pointing at the small grove.

"Looks to be."

"Then please stop when we get there."

"I don't—"

"You need only drop us there," Jennifer told Dannie, "then you can go on. We'll continue to Granite after Jesse's had time to recover."

"Ain't sure that's safe." Dannie looked to the north where the boiling smoke clouds continued to darken the sky. "Don't know what direction that fire might take."

"We'll be fine." Jennifer's mind was made up. "Jesse needs to rest, and bouncing around in the back of this wagon is not allowing her to do that. And the children are tired. We'll camp there."

Dannie frowned. "It's right next to the road. It ain't safe for ya."

"After what Jesse and I have been through, I'm sure we can manage spending a night or two by the side of this road. Besides," she looked along the length of the rough dirt path, empty from where they were all the way into Philipsburg, "it doesn't look to be too well traveled."

"Ain't safe. Best you stick with me to Granite." Dannie made no attempt to slow the wagon as it approached the thicket.

"Dannie, stop the damn wagon!" Jennifer ordered.

"Best do as she says," Jesse growled from directly behind Dannie's head. Hearing the wagon driver's reluctance to do as Jennifer asked, the woman had struggled to her feet and climbed up the inside of the wagon bed to reach the back of the wagon seat.

"Jesse!" Jennifer cried out, concerned about her wife overexerting herself in her weakened condition. "Get down from there before you fall."

"I'm fine, darlin'," Jesse wheezed, turning her attention back to Dannie. "Pull over or I'll climb up there and stop this team for you."

Dannie didn't much care for being ordered about, especially since she thought Jesse had already proven her poor judgment by taking a crippled wife and two babies into the wilderness. She thought about driving her elbow into the side of the rancher's head, sure that it would knock Jesse senseless, but she didn't. Having to explain to Leevie what had happened would be difficult. Dannie pulled on the reins and allowed the horses to slow to a stop at their own pace. When the wagon's motion finally stilled, she set the brake before climbing down to the ground. "You want ta stay out here, stay,"

By the time Dannie circled to the back of the wagon, Jesse was lifting the rear gate free. Resting the piece of wood against the inside of the wagon bed, she dropped to the ground, then turned to lift KC and Charley out. She carried the babies around to the side of the wagon and set them on the ground, then went to help Jennifer, who was already climbing down from the wagon seat.

Jennifer smiled as familiar hands encircled her waist. "Thank you, sweetheart." As soon as her feet touched the ground, she turned in Jesse's arms. "How do you feel?" she asked, tenderly brushing matted hair away from her wife's forehead.

"Tired and dirty," Jesse smiled, "but breathing is coming a little easier."

"Good."

"You sure you want to stay here?" Jesse asked as a piece of ash floated out of the sky and settled on Jennifer's nose. "She's right about the fire. And the road being so close."

"I know. But you're tired, the babies are tired, and I'm tired. And we don't know that being in Philipsburg or Granite is actually any safer than being out here. I want to be someplace I can just sit without moving." She looked at Jesse wistfully. "Can you understand that?"

Jesse gently leaned her forehead against her wife's. "Me, too. And someplace I can hold you."

Impatient to be moving on, Dannie interrupted. "You sure 'bout this?"

"Yes," Jennifer said, now wrapped in Jesse's arms. "Thank you for your help, Dannie." She smiled at the other woman. "Please tell Leevie not to worry about us. We'll be in Granite in a day or two, but first we're going to take some time to rest." She sighed. *Was it really only this morning when Jesse and I woke up to the smell of the approaching fire? It seems so much longer.* "We need some time to mend."

KC tugged on Jennifer's pant leg. "Momma."

Jennifer looked down at her daughter. "What, sweetie?"

"Cha-wie hungwy."

"I know," Jennifer told the exhausted girl. "I'll get something cooked up just as soon as we get a fire started. Okay?"

"Okay." KC nodded, then walked away from her mothers in search of firewood.

"Hold on there," Jennifer called to KC. "Wait for me to help, sweetie."

"If'n you're sure about staying put," Dannie told Jesse, "I'll be heading home."

"We're sure," Jesse said.

"Seems like a fool thing to do," Dannie muttered, watching the schoolteacher limp after her daughter.

Jesse bristled at the wagon driver's tone. "I appreciate you stopping to help Jennifer, but my wife is right about us being able to handle whatever might come up. We've done pretty well so far."

Dannie shrugged, then climbed back up into the wagon seat. "I can see how well you've done." She released the brake and slapped the reins over the horses' flanks.

Jesse glared at the driver as the wagon moved away. "Why you arrogant…"

"Sweetheart?" Jennifer returned with KC, both with arms full of firewood.

"Who the hell does she think she is, talking to us like that?"

Jennifer dropped the wood in order to wrap her arms around her angry wife. "It's been a long day, Jesse. Let it go, please."

Jesse looked at Jennifer. The dark circles under her eyes and the worry lines deeply etched across her brow reminded the rancher she had more important things to be concerned about than Dannie and her attitude. She kissed the tip of her wife's nose. "I'll get the fire started."

"I'll do that if you can get the packs off Boy so I can start cooking."

"Okay."

"Can you do it alone, Jesse?" Jennifer asked, troubled by the raspy sound of her wife's voice and her labored breathing.

"I'll give a holler if I can use some help." Jesse looked around the site. They were standing right at the edge of the path where it curved sharply as it left the side of the hill and turned to cross the valley floor on its way to Philipsburg. "Let's set camp a little further off the road." She nodded toward a depression closer to the thicket of trees where a shallow creek flowed. "Maybe over there in that low spot."

It took much longer than usual since she had to stop and rest several times, but Jesse managed to pull the packs and saddles off the horses. "Sorry, girl." She patted Dusty's neck. "Looks like you're gonna have to wait 'til tomorrow to get brushed down." Dusty whinnied, her head bobbing up and down as if she understood her mistress was struggling just to breathe.

Jennifer set a pot of water on top of a flat stone in the middle of the fire ring. Placing more pieces of firewood around it, she left it to heat. "KC, watch your brother while I help Mommy." She walked over to Jesse. "Sweetheart, go sit down."

"Got to get the tent up," Jesse rasped. It was warm enough to sleep on the ground, but with the air still full of ash and soot, she wanted her family protected as much as possible.

"Go sit down before you fall down." Jennifer's tone was firm. "I'll take care of the tent."

Jesse looked into her wife's determined eyes. "I can help," she offered weakly.

Jennifer cupped her hand against a soot-streaked cheek. "Please, go. You can barely stand up," she said softly.

Jesse nodded and gave in. Jennifer was right; it was taking all the energy she had just to remain upright. She went over to where KC and Charley were waiting for their mothers to finish setting up camp and eased her exhausted body to the ground, gasping for breath.

Jennifer pulled the tent off the pack, dragging it to the lowest area of the depression where the ground was the flattest. Unrolling the heavy canvas, she stretched out the sides. Picking up the longest support pole, she slipped it underneath the tent top and forced it upright, raising the center of the tent into position. She carried the rest of the support poles inside, working as quickly as she could to position them before stepping back outside. She found KC waiting for her.

"Mommy seeping," KC whispered.

Jennifer looked over to see Jesse collapsed on the ground. Charley had crawled over to his mother and was asleep in the crook of her arm. Jennifer looked down at her daughter, who was yawning and rubbing her eyes. "Seems we all need sleep a lot more than we need food right now," she murmured. She walked back to the packs and pulled their bedrolls free, then carried them into the tent and spread them out on the canvas floor. One more trip to the packs to retrieve clean sleeping shirts, diapers, and towels, and she was ready to get her family to bed.

"Sweetie," Jennifer told KC, "go inside and get those dirty clothes off while I get Charley."

"Okay," KC said tiredly, stepping into the tent. She began to pull off her clothes as soon as she was inside.

Jennifer carefully lifted Charley out of her sleeping wife's arms. She carried the baby into the tent, then returned for the pot of water heating in the fire, "Wash your face and hands, sweetie," she said as she placed the pot just outside the tent's opening. She stepped inside and knelt beside Charley to change his britches.

Naked, KC walked to the pot. She dipped her hands into the warm water, splashing it on her face. When that didn't seem to get much of the sooty grime off her skin, she bent over and dipped her face into the water — something she'd watch Jesse do many times. With her face underwater, she scrubbed vigorously with her little hands. Her head popped up moments later, water dripping off it back into the bucket. "Cean?" she asked, turning her face toward her mother.

Jennifer looked at the soot-smeared face. "Good enough for tonight." She grinned and handed the girl a towel. "We'll all have to take baths tomorrow. Can you get your nightshirt on?" she asked, dipping a cloth into the bucket to clean some of the grime off Charley.

"Yep." KC dried her face, then plucked the shirt off the bedroll and pulled the clean clothing over her head.

"Good girl." Jennifer smiled. "Now get into bed."

KC ran to Jennifer, wrapped her arms around her neck, and kissed her. "Wuv you, Momma," she said before she scampered back to the bedroll she would share with her brother and crawled inside.

"I love you, too, sweetie," Jennifer said, slipping Charley in beside KC. She leaned over and kissed both children. "Sweet dreams, my darlings."

"Mommy seep out dewe?" KC asked as Jennifer pushed herself up onto her feet.

"No. I'm going to go get her now."

"Good."

Jennifer stepped out of the tent. The sun was setting in the west, painting the sky blood red as its last rays of light shone through the thick layer of smoke hanging above the valley. She knelt beside Jesse, wincing at the sound of her wife's labored breathing. "Jesse," she said, gently rocking the sleeping woman's shoulder. "Sweetheart, wake up."

"Huh?" Jesse's eyelids fluttered open. "What's wrong?"

"Nothing." Jennifer smiled at her wife in the fading light. "But you need to get up so we can get you into the tent."

"Oh." Jesse rolled onto her side, then, bracing one hand against the ground, pushed herself up onto her hands and knees. She stayed in that position several minutes before she could force herself upright. Draping an arm over Jennifer's shoulders, she let her guide her into the tent.

Jennifer thought about undressing Jesse, who fell back asleep as soon as she was laid out on the bedroll but decided that removing her wife's boots would be enough for the night. With Jesse and the children settled in bed and fast asleep, she made one last trip outside before joining her family in rest.

Dusty walked up, nuzzling Jennifer's head as she pulled the rifle free of Jesse's saddle scabbard. She reached up and patted the mare's neck. "She'll be fine, girl. She just needs lots of rest for a while. Keep an eye on things out here tonight, okay? I don't think I'd wake up if an entire herd of buffalo ran through the camp." Dusty whinnied softly.

Jennifer yawned as she carried the rifle into the tent. After placing the rifle on the tent floor an arm's length above Jesse's head, Jennifer pulled off her dirty clothes. Dipping a towel into the bucket of cooled water, she washed what grime she could off of her face and arms, leaving the rest for the morning bath. Then she pulled the tent flap down and tied it securely. She made one last check on the babies before padding over to the bedroll and slipping in beside Jesse.

Jesse rolled over, curling her body around Jennifer's. "Love you," she mumbled.

Jennifer kissed the top of her wife's head. "I love you, too."

Jesse woke to find she was alone in the tent. The bright sunlight flooding through the opened tent flap and the hint of freshly cooked biscuits and fried bacon lingering in the air told her she had slept long past breakfast. She stretched out her long body, surprised at how tired she still felt. Her throat was dry and scratchy, and her chest ached. She figured that was from a combination of the smoke she had inhaled and all the coughing she had done since. Rising up on her elbows to look outside, she smiled at the sight that greeted her.

KC and Charley sat just outside the open flap, watching their mother sleep. As soon as Jesse's eyes met theirs, broad smiles spread across their worried faces.

"Momma," KC called to Jennifer, who was standing in the creek washing the clothes she had worn the day before. "Mommy wake."

"Thank goodness!" Jennifer limped to the creek bank. By the time she reached the tent, her children had already crawled inside the tent and were atop their mother. Jennifer smiled as she sat beside Jesse. "How are you feeling?"

"Tired, but okay." Jesse slipped a hand around Jennifer and pulled her down to her.

Jennifer melted into Jesse's embrace. "I was worried about you," she sniffled. "You coughed so much last night…I was so worried."

"Sorry, darlin'." Jesse turned her head to nuzzle her wife's hair, grinning when she smelled soap. "You've been busy this morning." Looking at KC and Charley, she realized they had also had baths, as their skin no longer wore the dark coloration of the day before. "And where are your boots?"

"I was washing clothes in the creek. Seemed easier just to take them off."

"Mommy." KC was crawling up Jesse's body. With knees on her mother's chest and hands braced against her shoulders, she looked down into Jesse's face. "We make biscuits. Cha-wie want eats dem aw but Momma say no. Momma say it fo' you."

Jesse squirmed as her daughter's sharp knees dug into her soft skin but chuckled at the serious expression on her daughter's face. "That was nice of Momma."

"You gets up. You eats. Okay?"

"Sure, Sunshine." Jesse tweaked the girl's nose, sending her into a fit of giggles and causing her to collapse onto her chest. "Ugh," she grunted.

"Sweetie..." Jennifer gently pulled KC closer to her, "get off Mommy until she feels better."

Charley crawled up to take KC's place. Draping his arms and legs over Jesse's sides, he laid his head between her breasts. Jesse placed a hand on the baby's back. "Guess if it ain't one, it'll be the other," she said to Jennifer.

"They were worried about you."

Jesse was quiet for a few minutes. "Seems like just once we'd be able to take a trip without something happening," she murmured, rubbing the baby's back. "Seems we've earned it."

"We're all safe," Jennifer whispered. "That's good enough for me."

Jesse turned to look into her wife's eyes, smiling at the love displayed in them. "Me, too."

KC bolted upright, looking hopefully from one mother to the other. "We eats?"

"I could use a little something," Jesse agreed. "Not to mention, a bath and a change of clothes. I must smell right awful."

"I like you just the way you are."

"Come on, Cha-wie." KC pushed herself to her feet and balanced for an instant on her momma's legs, then jumped to the tent floor. "Come on, Cha-wie," she called, running through the tent opening.

"Bleck." Charley watched his sister go but remained where he was.

"Seems Charley is starting to think for himself," Jesse said with a chuckle.

Jennifer laughed. "KC will be devastated."

"Cha-wie," KC's head popped back inside the tent, "come on."
"Bleck."

CHAPTER TWELVE

Charley's eyes fluttered open, and he rubbed at his nose. The acrid smoke that had been troubling him the past couple of days was still hanging heavy in the air. His head swiveled around when he heard the voices of his mothers.

"We should get up, darlin'," Jesse told Jennifer. The women had awakened some time earlier but had remained cuddled together in the bedroll.

"I know." Jennifer rolled over in Jesse's arms so she could face her and slipped her leg between her wife's.

Jesse smirked. "Don't go starting anything, Mrs. Branson. This ain't the place and I'd probably end up coughing anyhow." Her chest had started to clear but with all the smoke in the air, she still had trouble breathing at times. "Wish that fire would burn itself out so the air would clear."

Jennifer snuggled closer to Jesse. She loved the feel of their warm, naked bodies pressed together. "Do you think it's gone all the way to Sweetwater?"

"The fire or smoke?"

"Both."

"Smoke for sure. Hard to say with the fire, since we can't see which way it's moving."

"Your folks will be okay, won't they?"

"Sure. They know to clear out if it gets too close. Cattle are another thing. They'll probably scatter around the valley, maybe seek shelter in the box canyons."

"Will they be okay?" Jennifer knew how hard Jesse and her father had worked the past year to build the small herd. The thought of having to start all over with the cattle was bad enough, but what truly upset her was the likelihood their home could be destroyed again.

Jesse didn't want to think of the possibilities. "Let's just hope it doesn't go that way."

Charley rolled over onto his hands and knees. With a quick glance at his sleeping sister, he crawled out of the bedroll and across the floor of the tent. Jesse and Jennifer watched as the baby crawled on top of the bedroll toward them. He had a little difficulty finding something on which to brace his hands and knees, but he determinedly crawled forward until he reached his mothers. Climbing up on Jesse's hip, he tumbled over her body.

"Good morning, little man." Jennifer pulled her arm free of the bedroll to greet her son. "You're up early today." Charley grinned. "Not too often you have us all to yourself," she said, caressing his head.

"Funny he's awake and KC is still asleep." Jesse glanced over her shoulder at her daughter. "Usually it's the other way around." KC was stretched out on her back, one arm thrown out to the side and the other tucked under her chin.

Jennifer lifted her head just enough to peek over Jesse at their daughter. "I think she tuckered herself out yesterday with all the playing she did in the creek."

"Staying in camp was a good idea, darlin'." Jesse rolled her head back to look at Jennifer and reached up to cup her cheek. She traced her wife's lips with her thumb. "Think it did us all some good." She was pleased to see that the dark circles and worry lines had gone from the face she loved. Jennifer leaned into the caress, kissing Jesse's thumb. "We staying put or heading out today?" Jesse asked softly, her voice thick with emotion.

Cuddled next to the woman she loved, Jennifer would have preferred to stay exactly where she was forever. Nevertheless, she observed, "I suppose we should get to Granite. Leevie's probably worried sick about us."

Jesse frowned. She liked Leevie, but the thought of having to see the woman's lover again was not a pleasant one.

"What's wrong?" Jennifer asked, seeing the frown.

"I don't like Dannie," Jesse said bluntly.

"I know." Jennifer had her own misgivings about the rude wagon driver. "But it's only for a few days."

Jesse sighed. "Guess we need to be getting up then."

Jennifer held her wife in place and snuggled closer. "Dannie said Granite is only a couple of hours away. Let's wait until KC wakes up."

Jesse grinned. "That suits me just fine."

Jesse needed Jennifer's help getting the heavy packs back on Boy. The big draft horse stood patiently as the women worked. They were forced to take time between bursts of effort for Jesse to rest and regain her breath. It was close to midday before the horses were saddled.

"You ready, darlin'?" Jesse asked, placing KC on Dusty's saddle.

"I think so." Jennifer adjusted the carry sack so Charley was comfortable. She was again carrying the baby on her back. "Ready, Charley?" she asked, patting the baby's leg.

"Need help getting up?"

Jennifer smiled at Jesse. "I was just about to ask you the same thing."

"I think I can manage." Jesse walked over to help Jennifer mount Blaze. "Let's get you and Charley up there first."

"You'll tell me if you start feeling bad?" Jennifer asked, concerned that they might be leaving the camp too soon. "We can stop anytime and rest."

"I promise." Jesse leaned in for a quick kiss. "Now get up there so we can get going. Once we get to Granite, we can all take it easy for a couple of days."

With Jennifer mounted, Jesse pulled herself up onto Dusty's back. "Doing okay, KC?" She ruffled the girl's hair.

"Yep." KC tilted her head back to look up at her mother. "We goes?"

Jesse chuckled, urging the mare forward. "We goes."

"Jesse, don't you be encouraging her like that," Jennifer scolded as Blaze fell into step beside Dusty.

"Yes, darlin'," Jesse said, tickling KC.

An hour later, the women were riding down the main street of Philipsburg.

Tucked against the base of a large hill, the town was spread over the sides of several smaller hills. One- and two-story wooden and brick commercial buildings in various stages of construction lined the wide dirt street. The street itself was pitted with large hollows that the horses had to pick their way around or walk through.

"Why don't they do something about this awful street?" Jennifer asked as she watched a team of horses dip into one of the depressions, the wagon they were pulling tilting dangerously to the side.

"They will," Jesse said, guiding Dusty around another depression, "once they figure out there ain't no ore buried under it."

"You mean they've been digging up the street looking for gold?"

"Silver."

Several men working along the street watched the women pass, and Jesse was beginning to itch under the scrutiny. She pulled Dusty to a stop beside a man chewing on a cigar, watching them. "You ladies lost?" he asked, looking Jesse over carefully.

Not liking the man's eyes on her, KC shrunk back against her mother.

Rubbing the girl's tummy to reassure her, Jesse answered, "No, we're headed for Granite. Be obliged if you would point us in the right direction."

The cigar-chewing man thrust a thumb over his shoulder. "Down there. Take the road up to the top of the hill, you'll see a sign." When Jesse nodded her thanks, he spat in the dust. "Road ain't safe for ladies, 'specially ridin' on horseback," he added as Dusty walked away.

"And why is that?" Jennifer asked, holding Blaze in place.

"Freight wagons and stage won't stop for ya. You ain't careful, they'll run ya over."

Jennifer smiled at the man. "Thank you for the warning. We'll be careful."

"What's your business in Granite?" the man called after the women, who ignored the question.

Jennifer shuddered; she could still feel the eyes of the town's occupants on her back. When Blaze caught up with Dusty, she said, "I'm glad we aren't staying in Philipsburg."

"Don't expect much better in Granite," Jesse said, turning Dusty onto the side road the man had indicated. "Mining camps are all pretty much alike — rough men and spoiled women."

As Blaze turned to follow Dusty, Jennifer's eyes drifted down to the end of the town's main street, her attention drawn to a two-story wooden structure with a second-floor porch protruding over the boardwalk. A handful of women, all dressed in provocative clothing, were laughing and calling out to the men moving about on the street below them. The bits and pieces of the exchanges that Jennifer overheard left no doubt as to what services the women were offering. She wondered whether that was how the Silver Slipper had attracted customers before Jesse took over as owner.

The road climbed to the top of a steep hill, dipped slightly, then climbed up a gentler grade before coming to a crossroads. Near the junction, a wooden post slanted haphazardly in the ground. Painted in white on the plank of wood nailed to the post was the name of the town they were seeking. Jesse guided Dusty to the side of the road to allow room for a pair of heavily laden ore wagons to pass. Jennifer followed Jesse, covering Charley's face with her Stetson when the wagons rumbled by in a large cloud of dust.

"Darlin," Jesse said after the wagons had traveled far enough past them she didn't have to shout to be heard, "that man was right about one thing. The drivers of those wagons don't stop for anything once they get their teams moving. We'll need to stick to the inside of the curves; they need lots of room to turn the teams and wagons around them. When we hear a wagon coming, we'll need to get off the road if possible."

"Will it be possible?" Jennifer asked. She was more than a little frightened by the thought of coming face-to-face with one of the big ore wagons as they made their way up to Granite.

"Don't know." Jesse urged Dusty forward.

The road ran straight for about a half mile, the grade gentle but climbing steadily, then it curved sharply to the right and the incline became much steeper. Jesse directed the horses upward, keeping them as far to the side of the road as possible as it twisted up the mountain, winding around the slopes and switching directions so often it was hard to keep track of anything except that they were going uphill.

Rounding another hairpin turn, Jennifer couldn't imagine trying to maneuver a team of horses and an ore wagon around the sharp curves. She was developing a new respect for the drivers and muleskinners that managed to do so. Including the irascible Dannie.

Jesse heard the shouts of a wagon driver and the sound of horses straining. Spotting a wide space between the trees that bordered the road, she turned Dusty toward it. "Hurry, Jennifer," she called back to her wife. Blaze managed to bolt off the road just as a team of eight horses charged around the bend. Whip snapping over the horses' heads, the driver of the empty ore wagon yelled at the animals as they charged up the road. Once the team and wagon had passed, Jesse and Jennifer settled their jittery mounts.

"That was close," Jennifer sighed.

"Yep." Jesse frowned. "Should have asked that guy in Philipsburg if there was another way up this mountain."

"Don't you think he would have told us if there was?"

"Nope."

"Why not?"

Jesse shrugged. "Way it is," she muttered. "Ya don't answer what ain't asked. Come on, let's get going before another wagon comes by."

Jesse and Jennifer both breathed sighs of relief when they rounded a bend in the road and could see the mining activity on the mountain slope above them. It wasn't pretty, but it meant they had reached the end of their journey.

The road continued its steep ascent, and they rode past a large barn and stables belonging to the mining company, two churches, and a hotel before topping the crest. Spread out in front of the women was the town of Granite, built around the sides of a rounded gully stripped bare of the forest that had once covered the natural bowl.

"You know which way to go?" Jesse asked Jennifer, seeing that the road split in several directions.

The main road continued along the lip of the gulley and through the business district. One branch turned to the right and continued up the mountain to the mine itself, where a tall, wood beam headframe marked the location of the mouth of the deep shaft. A second branch dropped into the gully, providing access to the residential area of town.

Jennifer searched her memory for any details her friend had put in the letters she'd written. "Leevie said they had a place near the schoolhouse. It has a long rock wall in front of it."

"Well, I doubt it's up there." Jesse indicated the road that continued uphill. "And I doubt the school would be down that way," she said, looking at the beehive of activity around the commercial buildings. "Let's try this way." She nudged Dusty toward the middle branch.

They hadn't gone far when the road split again, a narrower branch dipping further down into the gully. Since the new branch wasn't wide enough for Dannie's team of horses, Jesse continued to lead her family along the street. They rode past cabins and shacks crowded together with little care for appearance or privacy. The few people they saw were mostly women and children; the men were probably working their shift at the mine or conducting business in town.

Off to her right, Jesse spotted the beginnings of a shoulder-high stone wall. In front of the wall, the street widened, providing ample room to park a team of horses and freight wagon and still allow passage of other traffic. A small house and larger barn occupied the ground above and behind the wall. She twisted in the saddle. "This look like what she described?"

Before Jennifer could answer, the door to the cabin burst open. "It's about time!" Leevie waved as she rushed outside. "I've been so worried about you two! If Dannie hadn't already agreed to take a load to Tower today, I would have sent her back after you."

Jennifer smiled at her friend. "Hi, Leevie."

Standing on top of the rock wall, Leevie said to Jesse, "Ride on up here. You can get up at either end of the wall. Is that little KC? My goodness, she has grown. Oh, that can't be Charley. Look how big he's gotten."

KC giggled as the words continued to flow out of Leevie while the horses walked around the end of the rock wall. "She funny, Mommy."

Jesse smiled at her daughter. "Hush. She's just excited to see your momma."

"Goodness, you get down from there and give me a hug," Leevie ordered as the horses stopped in front of the house. "I could not believe it when Dannie said she'd found you on the road to Philipsburg and then just left you there."

"Don't blame her," Jennifer said. "I didn't give her much choice."

"So I heard." Leevie chuckled. "I told her you were the one to watch out for. This big bad rancher of yours is all huff and no puff." She wrapped her arms around Jesse when she slid out of the saddle. "How are you?" she asked seriously, looking intently at the rancher.

"Better every day. Air's a bit cleaner up here." Jesse freed herself from the hug, then moved down the line of horses to help Jennifer off of Blaze.

"Don't depend on it staying that way. Soon as the wind shifts, we'll be covered in smoke too." Leevie winced at seeing Jennifer pull her cane out of the rifle scabbard. As the schoolteacher limped toward her, she mumbled, "Goodness, Jennifer, I know you wrote me all about it, but I never imagined—"

"Stop." Jennifer wrapped her arms around her distressed friend. "Don't you mind about my leg; I don't."

"But—"

"No," Jennifer said softly. "Talking about it doesn't change anything. I do everything I can and, what I can't, Jesse is always there to help out. So, don't be pitying me, please."

Leevie smiled sadly, glad to see her friend had not allowed her injury to ruin the life she enjoyed with her wife and children but angry that Jennifer's own father had caused her to suffer so horribly. "Let's go inside. I just made a fresh pitcher of lemonade and a batch of ginger cookies."

"I want cookie," KC told Jesse, who was lifting her down from Dusty.

"When don't you?" Jesse tickled her daughter. "Why don't you go inside, darlin'?" Jesse said, dropping KC to the ground. "I'll walk back to town and see about finding a place to board the horses and ask about getting a room in one of the hotels."

"Don't be silly," Leevie said. "You'll stay here with Dannie and me. There's plenty of room in the barn for your horses. And I wouldn't expect any decent lady to spend a night in town. If you thought Bannack was rough after dark, wait until the sun sets on Granite."

"Are you sure, Leevie?" Jennifer asked. "After all, we've grown in number since we stayed with you in Bannack."

Leevie smiled at the women. "I want you to stay here. It'll give us time to catch up, and you'll have a chance to get to know Dannie."

"Don't want to impose," Jesse muttered. "I'm sure Dannie needs the space for her team."

"Nonsense. Even with her team in there, the stalls are only half full. You go ahead and put your horses inside."

"All right," Jesse agreed grudgingly. She was thankful not to have to find a place in town; she was never comfortable with all the noise and activity. And having the horses where she could easily check on them would be nice, too. But the thought of accepting a favor from the insufferable freight driver didn't sit well with her. "Go on, darlin'," she told Jennifer. "I'll be in as soon as I get the horses rubbed down."

"I'll help," Jennifer offered immediately.

"I can do it."

"No, Jesse. You're wheezing again. I'll help."

"Mes he'p, too, Mommy," KC said, grabbing Blaze's reins and leading the horse away.

"It'll go faster, sweetheart," Jennifer said.

"All right."

"Well, let's get the work done, then," Leevie said, following KC. "Don't want to keep those cookies and lemonade waiting too long."

"Nope," KC agreed.

CHAPTER THIRTEEN

Jesse sat on the top of the rock wall holding Charley, the heels of her boots lightly tapping against the stones. KC sat next to her, her moccasin-clad feet matching the rhythmic movement of her mother. The sun, finally making an appearance over the mountain behind them even though it was late morning, was rapidly warming the air. They were waiting for Jennifer, who had accepted Leevie's invitation to walk to the schoolhouse located a short distance from the house.

Jesse was leisurely studying the layout of the town of Granite and the multiple rows of buildings occupying the rounded sides of the ravine. She was fascinated by the stores and other buildings on the near side of Main Street that were partially supported by stilts. With the street taking up most of the land along the rim of the gulley, it was the only way for structures bordering the busy street to find footing. On the other side of Main Street, business owners had the opposite but also unique problem of too much mountain, as the street had been cut right across the slope of the gulley. To make room for the stores, hotels, saloons, and other buildings, the earth had been carved out to accommodate the rear sections of the structures.

Behind Main Street, hastily thrown up shacks dotted what Leevie referred to as Whiskey Hill. Constructed without the benefit of solid foundations, most of the miners' cabins appeared to be on the brink of sliding down the slope into the backs of the businesses below.

The bowl-shaped gulley itself was crisscrossed with footpaths that were barely wide enough for two people to walk side by side. The paths wove their way through a variety of houses, shacks, and tents, home to most of Granite's citizens. She smirked at noticing that several feet below each row of homes was a corresponding row of outhouses, some tilting dangerously down slope.

A couple of streets below Leevie and Dannie's house, on the edge of the residential area, was a large two-story wooden structure that was neighbored by a half dozen saloons not able to squeeze onto Main Street. Well-worn dirt paths led down to it from the business district. Seeing the men entering and leaving by the front door and the women who greeted and bade them goodbye, she instantly identified the activity taking place inside the building. She wasn't surprised to see the house of ill repute in

Granite; every mining camp had its share of saloons and prostitutes.

"Momma, what dat?"

Jesse swung her head around to look where her daughter was pointing. "What, Sunshine?"

"Dat."

"Dat" was a granite boulder rising out of the ground about three hundred feet down the ravine. "Looks like a great big rock," Jesse said.

"We go dewe?"

Jesse chuckled. "Why would you want to go down there?"

"Cha-wie wants ta pway."

"Seems a might far to go just so you can play." Jesse smiled. "Can't you play up here?"

KC twisted around to look behind her. "S'pose." She shrugged, her head cocked to one side as she imagined the possibilities.

"Good." Jesse ruffled the girl's hair. "'Cause I'm not sure I could make it back up once we got down there. Maybe after a day or two, when my breathing comes a bit easier."

KC twisted back around. Using her hands to boost her body along, she scooted closer to Jesse and leaned against her. "We wait."

Jesse shifted Charley to sit on her right thigh so she could wrap her left arm around her daughter. "Thanks."

Dannie walked back along Main Street toward the junction of streets at the start of town. She had spent the morning unsuccessfully asking every business owner in town about the possibility of carrying their freight up from Philipsburg. Desperate to make more money so she and Leevie could stay in Granite and be together, she was determined to talk the foreman of the mining company into signing her on as a regular driver.

Leaving Main Street, she walked up the steep grade that led to the mine at the top of the mountain. Fancifully named Broadway, the wide street provided the only access to the area below the mine where mining company buildings stood side by side with homes, hotels, and churches. She left Broadway when she reached the street officially named Magnolia but generally referred to as Silk Stocking Row by the townsfolk because along its length were the finely constructed brick and stone houses of the mining company's highest paid employees.

Dannie had taken only a few steps when she spied the impressive two-story stone structure that served double duty as office and residence of the foreman and his family. A flight of stairs in back provided access to the office on the second floor, while the first floor living quarters were accessed by a door facing Silk Stocking Row. Circling around to the back, Dannie took a deep breath to calm her nerves before climbing the steps to the office and pushing the door inward.

When the door opened, the foreman looked up from his desk, which occupied a corner of the large open room to take advantage of sunlight coming through both a window on the side and a pair of dormer windows on the building's front. He acknowledged her with a curt nod.

"Afternoon, Mr. Garrison."

"Afternoon." He waited for her to provide a reason for her intrusion.

"I know you're short of drivers—"

"I don't have any business for you."

"Signs in town say different, Mr. Garrison."

"I can't hire a woman. Good day."

"I don't know what me being a woman has got to do with anything. Signs say you need wagons and teams; I've got both," Dannie persisted.

"I can't hire you."

"I hear you've been in town every day complaining you don't have enough wagons to haul supplies up from Philipsburg. And you tell me you don't have business for me?"

"Everyone knows a woman can't drive a team of horses," the man grumbled. When Dannie made no movement toward the door, he added, "I've got work to get back—"

"*I* drive a team, you fool!" Dannie said, her frustration rising.

"Driving a team in the valley ain't the same as on the mountain."

"I live on this mountain, and I've driven my team up and down almost every one of its damned roads."

Garrison leaned back in his chair, studying the woman standing in front of his desk. He knew Dannie owned a wagon and team and, despite what he had just said, he knew she was a good driver and an honest one. But he also knew that if he hired her, he'd have to explain his decision to the company's owners and stockholders in St. Louis. "I can't hire you."

"I need the money," Dannie explained. "Please. I'll take the runs no one else wants."

"I'm sorry. I'd like to help you, but it's not up to me. The mine owners make the rules and they'd never understand why I hired a woman with all the men around here begging for work."

"Can't ya tell them those men don't drive wagons?"

"Sorry." Garrison deliberately returned to his work, effectively precluding any further conversation.

Dannie turned away, her shoulders slumping as she stepped outside and descended the wooden steps. Walking to the front of the building, she took a moment to stand on the street and take in her surroundings.

Silk Stocking Row stretched off to her left, leading to a maze of streets and narrow lanes where the mine's other offices, workshops, warehouses and storage sheds, company store, and pay office were located. She looked across to the Philipsburg road where freight wagons regularly appeared around the last sharp bend on their way to unload their cargos along Main Street or continued up Magnolia to the mining operation. Between her and the road stood the company's two-story hospital and the adjacent home for the resident doctor. The company barn, stables, and blacksmith shop occupied the low ground between the hospital and the road. Without looking, Dannie knew that several hundred feet up the side of the mountain behind her was the mine and the immense structure where the stamp mills worked around the clock to separate ore from the rock dug out of the mountain. She knew there would be wagons lined up at the loading chutes ready to take that ore down the mountain to the processing plant near Philipsburg. Everywhere she looked screamed money, but she wasn't allowed to share in even a little portion of it.

No sense putting off the inevitable, Dannie thought. The trip she'd made to Tower the day before had barely paid enough to buy feed for her horses. With most of the business owners in both Granite and Philipsburg almost as reluctant to hire her as Garrison, Dannie realized her stay in Granite and her dream of living with her lover were at an end. She sighed as she began the walk back to their house. *Best go home and break the news to Leevie.*

"Are you sure that's what you want to do, Jennifer?" Leevie asked. They were sitting on a bench in the empty schoolyard, the students having been called inside by their teacher.

"I'm tired of spending my days with other people's children; I want to be with my own."

"What about Jesse? Have you told her?"

"Not yet, but I don't think she'll mind. What with the Silver Slipper, the dress shop, and the ranch, there just isn't enough time to take care of everything any more. I'm sure she'll be just as happy to have me at home as being there will make me."

Leevie smiled. "It's tempting, Jennifer; it really is. I knew I shouldn't have taken so long to accept Dannie's offer to come here. By the time I finally made it, there were many other women in town qualified to be teachers and looking for work. Now, as you heard from Sarah," she referred to the Granite schoolteacher who had spent the past hour talking with them before the students returned for their afternoon classes, "there's not much chance of me being offered one of the teaching positions Dannie was told would be available. And I know she is having a hard time finding jobs, even though she keeps assuring me everything is all right." Leevie sighed. "Thing is, just like you want to be with Jesse, I want to be with Dannie. I don't think I could live away from her."

"And you won't have to. That's what makes this so perfect," Jennifer said excitedly. "Jesse's been helping Ed out with his deliveries, but she really hates it when she has to be gone overnight. And now that Billie and Ruthie have the baby, Billie doesn't like to be away any more than Jesse does."

Leevie grinned. "So if Dannie was there, she could make the deliveries."

Jennifer nodded. "Yes. And she would have no shortage of jobs because Sweetwater doesn't have anyone but Ed to deliver freight when it comes in from Bozeman. And he can't leave the store."

"It's perfect."

"Do you think Dannie would be willing to move to Sweetwater? It will be different from what you're used to after being here and in Bannack. I mean, she's a little rougher than most folks in Sweetwater," Jennifer said timidly. She knew little about Leevie's lover, but what she did know wasn't all that favorable.

Leevie laughed. "Don't let Dannie fool you. She's rough on the outside, but I'm thinking that she and Jesse aren't too different on the inside. Besides, she has to appear rough, otherwise the other freighters don't take her seriously."

"I suppose she and Jesse have that in common, too."

Leevie nodded her understanding of Jesse's relationship with the other Sweetwater ranchers, something Jennifer had written about in her letters. "I think Dannie will be happy any place she can find work and we can be together," Leevie said, crossing her fingers. "But let's get back so I can ask her."

"And I can break the news to Jesse." Jennifer figuratively had her own fingers crossed, hoping her wife wouldn't be too upset with her desire to give up teaching.

After feeding the babies, and bored with just sitting and waiting for Jennifer to return, Jesse decided to muck out the horse stalls. Even with the doors open at both ends of the building, it was hot inside the barn. The rancher paused in her chore to wipe the sweat off the back of her neck with her kerchief. KC and Charley were napping on a blanket spread out in the shade in front of one of the doorways to take advantage of a light breeze blowing up the gulley from the valley. Jesse was glad to see that neither was showing signs of waking as she still had a bit of work to do.

"What are you doing?" Dannie asked, stomping in through the doorway at the opposite end from the sleeping children. She wasn't happy to see the rancher cleaning out the stalls, something she had been meaning to find the time to do for days.

Jesse returned to the work, tossing another shovelful of horse biscuits into the wheelbarrow. "Not used to sitting around all day doing nothing."

"I can take care of my own barn."

"Never said ya couldn't." Jesse turned to face the angry wagon driver. "Just helping out. Looked as if you could use some."

"I can take care of my own affairs," Dannie spat. "I don't need the likes of you showing up here and trying ta say I can't."

"What the hell is that supposed to mean?" Jesse leaned the shovel against a stall partition, not wanting it to become a handy weapon if Dannie became more irrational. "I said I was just trying to help. Don't know why you're so upset over it. Someone offered to muck out my barn, I sure wouldn't turn them down."

"This ain't your barn."

"I know that."

"You think 'cause you've got things your way in Sweetwater you can just walk in and take over here? Well, ya can't."

Jesse reached for the canteen she had hung on a post earlier. "I don't know what kind of burr you've got stuck under your saddle, but I wish you'd pull it out. I thought I'd muck out the barn to repay you and Leevie for puttin' us up." She took a long swallow of water. "Hell, woman, ever since we first met, you've been acting like I've done something wrong."

"Everything always goes right for you, don't it?" Dannie growled. "Ya win a poker game and end up in business. You buy a ranch. You find a couple of young 'uns. Everything comes easy for ya. 'Cept your wife's a cripple—"

Jesse had her hands around Dannie's throat, strangling off her next words. "Jennifer ain't no cripple!" she snarled in the other woman's face. "And if you call her that again, I'll—"

"Jesse!" Jennifer rushed toward them, Leevie on her heels. After finding the house empty, they had been walking to the barn when they heard the ugly confrontation going on inside. "Let her go," she said as she reached her wife's side. She had never seen Jesse so angry and was afraid she would seriously injure the woman she had in a chokehold.

Dannie's eyes bulged, both from a lack of air and from the fury in the rancher's eyes. She felt Jesse's hands trembling as she tightened her grip.

"Please, Jesse," Jennifer whispered. "Please, let her go."

"Mommy?"

Jesse froze as KC's arms wrapped around her leg. She looked down to see her daughter looking wide-eyed back at her. Instantly, her grip relaxed and her hands dropped to her sides.

Leevie ran up to Dannie. "Are you all right?" Dannie nodded, gasping for breath. She rubbed her neck to ease the burning sensation that lingered. Angry red marks stood out on her skin where the choking fingers had been moments before. "What did you say to her?" Leevie asked, her tone more accusatory than she had intended.

Dannie looked at her lover. She slowly backed away, shaking her head. "Even you think she's better'n me," she mumbled.

"No, Dannie!" Leevie cried. "That's not what I meant."

She reached out to wrap her arms around Dannie, but Dannie swiped at them, knocking them aside. "No point in me sticking around if that's the case." She spun around and marched toward the doorway. "Do what you want with the horses and wagon," she yelled as she walked out into the sunlight. "I don't have the money to keep 'em anyway."

"Dannie!" Leevie screamed. "Where are you going?"

When Leevie caught up with her and grabbed her arm, Dannie growled, "Leave me be, woman. I... Just leave me be." She snatched her arm free and turned back toward town.

Jennifer grabbed Jesse's arm. "Jesse, what happened here?"

Instead of answering, Jesse knelt down to console a whimpering KC, whose arms were wrapped tightly around her leg. "It's okay, Sunshine."

When Jesse stood, lifting her into her arms, KC snuggled against her. "You ye-win'," she sniffled.

"I know." Jesse hugged the distressed child. "I'm sorry."

"Jesse?" Jennifer repeated. "What happened?"

"I'm not sure."

"You were choking her."

"She said something she shouldn't have," Jesse muttered. "We both said some things we shouldn't have. I shouldn't have done what I did."

"She's gone." Leevie stared at the empty opening at the end of the barn, tears flowing down her cheeks. "She's really gone."

Jesse handed KC to Jennifer, then joined Leevie. "Where would she go?" Leevie looked blankly at the rancher. "To blow off the steam she's got built up," Jesse explained. "Where would she go?"

"I'm not sure."

"She's on foot. Is there someplace in town?" Jennifer suggested.

"Maybe Donegal's. It's the saloon next to the newspaper office."

"What are you going to do?" Jennifer asked as Jesse started to walk away.

"Find her," Jesse told her wife. "See if I can work this out between us and then bring her home."

Jennifer limped after her wife, who stopped and waited for her. "Sweetheart, are you sure you should?"

Jesse shrugged. "No. But I think she's got some things she needs to talk out. She's been keeping them bottled up inside and that ain't good. Maybe she'll..."

"Talk to you?"

"Maybe."

Jennifer smiled. "And you know this because you do the same thing, don't you?"

Jesse grinned. "Used to. 'Fore I met you." She leaned close, kissing Jennifer. "Stay put until I get back."

"Bring her home," Leevie told Jesse.

"Don't worry. She's got a hard head...like me, but she's not going to walk away from the woman she loves."

Jennifer watched Jesse leave. "Damn."

"Think she'll find Dannie?" Leevie asked, wiping tears from her face.

"She won't stop until she does. She's right about them both having hard heads. And about them loving us."

"What do you think Dannie said to her?"

"I don't know," Jennifer answered honestly. But she was sure that whatever it was had something to do with her or the babies because there was nothing else that would cause her wife to react so violently. "Whatever it was, it's not important," she said. "Help me with Charley, and let's go back to the house. I bet KC would like a glass of your lemonade."

Jesse walked almost the full length of Main Street before she located Donegal's saloon, a rough-hewn log cabin squeezed between a two-story hotel and the newspaper office. Located on the gully side of the street, the saloon was one of the few buildings that didn't hang out over the ravine needing to be propped up by stilts. She was thankful for that as she stepped directly from the boardwalk through the open doorway, exchanging bright sunlight for the dark interior of the one-room building.

The saloon's furnishings were sparse. Half a dozen tables and twice as many chairs were situated about the room, and a curious bartender watched her from behind a plank of wood resting on two empty flour barrels. Oil lamps hanging from the log walls and the roof beam provided the only illumination in the windowless cabin. Most of the patrons were miners who eyed her suspiciously.

Jesse stood just inside the door looking for Dannie. Spotting a figure hunched over a table in the shadows of a back corner, she walked across the room.

"Go away," Dannie grumbled when Jesse pulled over an unoccupied chair from another table and sat down.

"Can't."

"Why not?"

"Jennifer would beat me to within an inch of my life if I didn't bring you back."

Dannie glared up at Jesse. "Thought you wore the pants."

Jesse laughed. "If you haven't noticed, Jennifer is quite fond of wearing britches."

"You drinkin' or talkin'?" the bartender called over to the women.

"Bring me another beer," Dannie yelled back.

"You have any milk?" Jesse asked, smiling when the other patrons guffawed.

"Hell, no."

"Then make it two beers."

The women were silent until their drinks were served, and the bartender retreated back behind his plank of wood.

"Look, I'm sorry," Jesse said. "I shouldn't have done what I did."

"Why did you?" Dannie rubbed her bruised neck, still nervous over the raw temper the rancher had displayed.

"I don't like people making Jennifer out to be less than what she is." Jesse took a swallow of the warm beer.

Dannie nodded. "I was wrong calling her what I did."

"You were. Mind telling me what the rest of what you said was about?"

"Forget it." Dannie gulped down half her beer, then raised the almost empty mug for the bartender to see.

"I'd rather not."

"Why? It don't concern you."

"Seems to me that we're going to be seeing a lot more of each other if our wives have anything to say about it. We might as well get all this out now."

"Me and Leevie ain't married."

Jesse grinned. "You should be."

"You got money to pay for these, Dannie?" the bartender asked, setting two fresh mugs of beer on the table.

"I should be picking up a load tomorrow," the freight driver muttered.

The bartender started to pick up the mugs. "Leave them." Jesse reached into her pocket to retrieve some coins. "This should take care of us for a while."

Her earlier anger returning, Dannie's eyes narrowed when she saw Jesse nonchalantly hand the payment to the bartender. "You got it made, don't you?" she sneered.

Jesse looked at the woman, puzzled by her sudden change in mood. "You really think that?" she asked. "Dannie, I know from where you're sitting it probably looks like I got it easy, but my life ain't always been so rosy. And what it is today is mostly due to hard work and Jennifer."

Dannie gulped her beer, draining the mug before slamming it down on the table. "I work hard," she muttered. "Worked a lotta years to afford me a team and wagon, but men don't want to hire me 'cause I'm a woman. You don't have that problem."

Jesse laughed. "Damn, is that what this is all about? You think I've got it easier than you in that department? Hell, Dannie, half the ranchers in the Sweetwater Valley wouldn't do business with me, at first. 'Ain't fittin' for a woman to own a ranch,' they'd tell me. 'Ain't fittin' for a woman to own a saloon.' 'Ain't fittin' for a woman to drive a wagon.' Bet you've heard that one a time or two."

Dannie nodded, staring into her beer mug.

"Just because they say it, don't make it true." Jesse frowned. "After I took over the Slipper, folks would cross the street rather than have to talk to me. If it wasn't for Ed, who could have cared less if I was a woman or a man just so long as I paid my tab at his store, I never could have made a go of the Slipper. Once I turned out the card sharks and working girls, the boarding rooms spent more time collecting dust than customers. And about the only folks Bette Mae was feeding in the dining room was Ed and me. But word slowly got 'round that the Slipper had clean beds and good food, and folks started coming just to check things out. Lucky for me, they decided to stick around." Jesse took a swig of beer.

"Business finally got good enough for me to buy a rundown cabin and some grassland that I could call a ranch. Only problem was, none of the other ranchers would sell me any cattle. Had to talk 'til I was plumb tired of talking to convince one of 'em to sell me a dozen cows for twice what they was worth. Still, he refused to sell me a bull to breed 'em." Jesse twisted around in her chair, signaling the bartender that they needed their mugs refilled.

"Hell, Dannie, only thing ever to come easy to me was my love for Jennifer. She had that from the minute she stepped off the stage, though it took me a bit to wrangle that out. And I probably never would have if she hadn't prodded me some." Jesse smiled at the memory of those first few weeks she'd shared with the newly arrived schoolteacher and discovering she was in love with the ginger-haired woman. She turned her attention back to Dannie. "So, what burr got hooked onto you?"

"I'm busted," Dannie admitted. "I love Leevie; I don't know how to tell her. Granite is the first place we've managed to live together. It'll break her heart if I have to leave her behind and go someplace else to find work."

"What if she could come with you?" Jesse asked as two more mugs of beer were left on the table. Dannie looked at her dubiously. "Sweetwater needs someone to haul freight. Ed's got more supplies arriving every day for the mining camps and ranches. It's too much for me and Billie to keep up with, especially since I've got the ranch and the Slipper to worry about, and now Billie's got a young 'un and doesn't want to be leaving town much. You have a wagon and team; Ed would put you to work soon as you rode into town."

"What about Leevie?"

Jesse thought a long moment before answering. Deciding she could explain her reasons to her wife later, she continued. "I've been wanting to ask Jennifer to stop teaching. We need her at home. She'd be more willing to do it if she had someone to replace her, someone she knew would do right by the school and the young 'uns there."

Dannie thought over the offer, then shook her head. "Can't do it. Can't just up and take Leevie to a new town. I need money to get a place for her, and I don't have any."

"You don't need any, least not right off. You could room at the Slipper to start with. Town will pay Leevie for her teaching soon as the new term starts. After that, you can find someplace better for the two of you."

"Sure the town wants more of us around?" Dannie asked seriously.

"More of *us*?"

Dannie leaned across the table and lowered her voice. "Ya know — women living as if we was married. We've tried to keep it quiet here so's not to cause trouble, but folks figured it out soon enough. Most haven't taken too kindly to us."

"I'm not saying it'll be easy. You'll get the stares and looks from some, same as Jennifer and me. But if you pay them no mind, you can go about your business."

"What about the ranchers? They gonna be wanting me driving a wagon onto their places?"

"Probably not. But they need their supplies, and they don't like sending a cowhand to town to get them. They usually end up at the Oxbow too drunk to remember what they were sent to town to do. If you're workin' for Ed, most won't question it."

"What about you?"

"What about me?"

"You gonna want me living 'round ya?"

Jesse drank down the last of her beer. "I've got nothin' against you, Dannie, and I like Leevie, she's good for Jennifer. But no one…" she set the empty mug down and glared at the freight driver to make sure her point was being made, "no one talks about Jennifer, or KC, or Charley, like you did and expects me to let it go."

Dannie nodded. "Can't argue with you 'bout that. I feel the same about Leevie. Speaking of…" She downed the last of her beer. "Guess we should be getting on home."

"Probably a good idea." Jesse smiled. "They're most likely worried about what ditch we've fallen into after beating the stuffing outta each other."

Dannie laughed, then sobered. "Be nice to have some good news to tell Leevie for once."

"You'll come to Sweetwater?"

"Don't see any reason not to." Dannie offered her hand across the table to Jesse. "You mind if we start this meetin' thing all over?"

Jesse laughed, taking the outstretched hand and squeezing it. "Glad to meet ya. I'm Jesse Marie Branson."

"Dorothy Annabelle Northly."

Jesse snorted. "That's where Dannie comes from?"

"And if you ever tell anyone, I'll rip your tongue out. Not even Leevie knows my given name."

"She won't hear it from me." Jesse snickered as she stood up, then quickly dropped her hands to the table, gripping the edge and hanging on while the room spun around her. "Fact is, after what I just had to drink, I doubt I'll remember it by morning." She hadn't consumed a single beer in months and was pretty sure the last time she'd had more than one at the same sitting was long before she'd met Jennifer. She dropped back into her chair. "Maybe we should sit a spell longer before we head back."

"Want another?" Dannie asked, holding up an empty mug.

"Why not. If I have to be sitting here, might as well enjoy myself."

"What's that?" Jennifer asked, hearing the sound of rowdy laughter coming from the street in front of the house.

"Just a couple of drunks on their way home," Leevie explained. She was used to the nightly activity of intoxicated miners making their way home after spending the evening in one or more of the twenty plus saloons on Main Street.

Jennifer turned her head to hear better; something was oddly familiar about one of the slurred voices. And they seemed to be getting closer to the house. "You don't think…"

"It couldn't be," Leevie said, although she too recognized one of the voices.

Both women hurried to the door, opening it just as Jesse and Dannie stumbled up to the porch.

"Uh, oh," Dannie whispered loudly when she saw the look on her lover's face.

"Jesse, you're drunk," Jennifer said as indignantly as possible through the grin she wore.

"Sorry, darlin'," Jesse said, tightening her hold on Dannie to keep herself upright.

Jennifer bit her lip to keep from laughing at the pair of swaying women who were dangerously close to falling into a tangled heap. "Well, I certainly hope you two got your differences worked out."

Jesse grinned crookedly. "We did. We're moving ta Sweetwater," she slurred, slowly collapsing to the ground, her rubbery legs no longer able to support her. Somehow Dannie remained standing, although she was weaving unsteadily.

Jennifer stepped outside to stand over Jesse, looking down at the disheveled pile of limp limbs that was her wife. She giggled. "Guess we know where you're sleeping tonight."

"Yes, darlin'." Jesse curled into a ball. "Love you."

"Guess she does wear the pants," Dannie snickered. "Let's go ta bed," she said, reaching for Leevie.

"Oh, no you don't." Leevie stepped away from her lover's grasp. "You can sleep out here with her."

"But, Leevie..." Dannie whined.

"Come on, Jennifer," Leevie turned her back to Dannie, "let's get inside where it's warm, and we can eat some of those ginger cookies waiting for us."

Dannie swallowed hard at the mention of food. Her stomach starting to tumble, she swallowed again.

Returning inside the house, Leevie said to the waiting children in a voice louder than necessary, "I bet you two would like a nice big glass of milk and a warm ginger cookie, wouldn't you?" She slammed the door shut.

Dannie's fist flew up to her mouth as she looked around for someplace to empty the contents of her rebelling stomach. Staggering to the stone wall, she dropped to her knees and retched over the edge.

Jesse smirked. And that was the last thing she did before she fell asleep.

CHAPTER FOURTEEN

"Whe-uh Mommy?" KC asked, lifting her arms above her head so a clean shirt could be dropped over it. She was sitting on the bedroll spread out on the floor where she had spent the night with her mother and brother.

"Outside." Jennifer giggled. She had checked on Jesse earlier in the morning and found her wife still curled up in a ball near in front of the house.

"She seeping?"

"Yes, sweetie."

KC looked over her mother's shoulder. The sun was shining brightly through the windows. "It wate."

"Yes, it is." Thinking, Jennifer sucked on her lower lip. "Maybe you and Charley would like to go see if she's awake."

KC nodded. "We goes."

"Let me get your moccasins on first."

"Okay." KC leaned back. Supporting herself on her hands, she held both feet up in the air.

"You seem to be taking this awfully well," Leevie said from across the room where she was frying bacon.

"Well," Jennifer pushed herself up off the floor, "it's the first time I've ever seen Jesse drunk. And to be honest, I'd much rather she came home drunk than shot or beat up. Besides, after those two get through with her, I doubt she'll do it again any time soon." She watched KC hold the door open for Charley to crawl outside.

"Think they can take care of Dannie, too?" Leevie asked, looking out the window. Her lover was sound asleep on the top of the rock wall, precariously close to the edge.

"Don't you think you should go wake her up before she rolls off?"

"No." Leevie removed the bacon from the pan, then poured several scrambled up eggs into the hot cast iron. "This isn't the first time she's come home drunk. Maybe if she falls off, she'll stop doing it."

"Is it a problem for her?" Jennifer asked, rolling up the bedroll.

"Just when she gets frustrated over not being able to find work. What do you think Jesse meant last night when she said *we're* moving to Sweetwater? I didn't think you'd talked to her yet."

"I haven't. I have no idea what she meant." Jennifer placed the roll of blankets next to the wall where they would be out of the way during the day. "I wish she would wake up, so I could ask."

"Don't think she's going to have much choice about that." Leevie laughed as KC and Charley approached their sleeping mother.

KC tiptoed toward Jesse. "Mommy seeping, Cha-wie," she whispered to the baby crawling beside her. "We needs be quiet." She held a finger up to her mouth to emphasize her caution.

Charley looked up at his sister and frowned. He looked at his mother, who had rolled over onto her back, an arm slung over her eyes to block out the morning sun. He liked to sit on his mommy's stomach and bounce, and right now she was in the perfect position for that. Ignoring his sister, he started crawling again.

"Cha-wie," KC whispered at her brother. "Cha-wie, you gots ta stay put."

"Bleck." Charley shook his head, his hands and legs still moving forward.

KC started to run after her brother, more concerned with stopping him than disturbing her sleeping mother. The baby reached Jesse first. Swinging a hand out to her shirt, he grabbed a fistful of material to pull himself up. "Cha-wie, no," KC cried out, just as the toe of her moccasin caught a root poking out of the ground. Unable to stop herself, she stumbled a few steps forward, arms flailing as she tried to regain her balance. Charley ducked, and his sister flew past him to land squarely on top of their mother.

"Oof." Jesse jerked awake, unsure of where she was or what was squirming about on her chest.

While KC struggled to untangle her arms and legs, Charley pulled himself up to sit on Jesse's belly, his legs hanging over her sides.

"What?" Jesse muttered, her tongue sticking to the roof of her cotton-dry mouth. She tried again. "What's goin' on?"

Hearing his mother's voice, Charley giggled and started bouncing.

KC finally got herself turned right side up. She bent down, nose-to-nose with her mother. "Hi, Mommy. We makin' bacon and eggs. You hungwys?"

Feeling the bile rising up her throat, Jesse clamped her jaws shut. "Charley," she hissed through her clinched teeth, "please stop that."

Encouraged when his mother spoke to him, Charley increased his bouncing.

KC pushed herself up on her knees, the sharp bones poking into Jesse's ribs. She twisted around to tell her brother, "Mommy says stop, Cha-wie."

"Bleck." Charley wrinkled up his nose, refusing to obey his sister.

A shadow fell across Jesse, and she looked up to see Jennifer standing over her. "Help me," she moaned pitifully.

Jennifer chuckled. "KC, go wake up your Auntie Dannie."

"Okay." KC pushed herself up, her feet replacing her knees on Jesse's chest. "I be back, Mommy," she shouted, jumping to the ground.

"Charley, stop bouncing," Jennifer softly told the baby, who immediately ceased his movements.

"Thank you," Jesse groaned.

"Did KC tell you Leevie is cooking up a batch of bacon and eggs for breakfast?" Jennifer asked cheerfully.

Jesse forced the bile down as she glared up at her wife. "You're enjoyin' this, ain't ya?" she asked woefully.

"Yep." Jennifer laughed. She bent down to pick up Charley but found herself caught in Jesse's grip instead.

"Jennifer Stancey Branson," Jesse growled, wrapping her arms around her wife's waist and pulling her down beside her, "I never knew you could be so wicked."

"Make me sleep alone while you're lying out in the dirt like some common drunk..." Jennifer growled right back. "You haven't seen the end of my wickedness."

"What the hell!"

Jesse and Jennifer looked in the direction of the yell to see KC standing on the top of the rock wall, bent at the waist as she looked over the edge. "Oops." KC's hands came up to her mouth in surprise. "Auntie Dannie, yous okay?"

"Can this day get any worse?" Jesse dropped her head back, groaning when it connected with the hard ground.

"Bleck." Charley giggled, renewing his bouncing.

Jennifer buried her face against Jesse's shoulder, her body shaking with laughter.

"Why didn't you just tell me you wanted me to stop teaching?" Jennifer asked, washing Jesse's back.

The rancher sat in the tub on the back porch of Dannie and Leevie's house. A curtain was hung around the tub, providing some privacy from the surrounding homes. KC and Charley were playing on the porch next to Jennifer's stool.

"Didn't think it was my place to ask you to give up something you loved," Jesse admitted.

"Sweetheart, I love you and the children much more than I do teaching." Jennifer rinsed soap off her wife's smooth skin. "You should have just asked."

Jesse smiled. "Yeah?"

Jennifer tapped her finger against the tip of her wife's nose. "Yeah. Now let me get your hair washed. I don't even want to think about what might be crawling around in it."

KC stood up. Grabbing onto the rim of the tub and standing on her tiptoes to see, she cocked her head to one side looking at her mother. "Mommy?"

"Yes, Sunshine?"

"You gots bugs?"

"No, I don't have—" Jesse's protest was cut short when Jennifer poured a bucket of cold water over her head.

"You sure about this?" Leevie asked Dannie. The women were sitting atop the stone wall, waiting Dannie's turn with the tub.

"Ain't got much choice," Dannie said. "Can't get enough work here to keep the horses in feed."

"That's not much of an answer, Dannie."

Dannie looked at her lover. "Yes, I want to do it. If what Jesse said is true, it'll be what we always hoped for — you can teach and I can drive my wagon. And..." she smiled shyly, "we can be together."

"It does sound perfect, doesn't it?" Leevie rested her head against Dannie's shoulder.

"Yes." Dannie started to slip her arm around her lover but stop abruptly, wincing at the pain that shot through the bruised limb. "Damn," she groaned, rubbing her shoulder.

"At least it isn't broken."

"No thanks to that—"

"Dannie," Leevie warned.

"Hmpft. Who told her she could call me *Auntie*?" Dannie grumbled. "Makes me sound like an ol' biddy just waitin' to die."

"She likes you." Leevie chuckled. Once KC was let loose on Dannie, the girl seemed to enjoy pestering the cantankerous woman.

"Well, I ain't so sure I like her."

"Sure you do. You know why?"

"Why?"

"Because I bet you were a lot like her when you were a young 'un."

"You do, huh?"

"Yes."

"What if I say I wasn't?"

"I wouldn't believe you."

"Auntie Dannie," KC ran around the corner of the house, "Mommy says yous needs take baff."

"She does, does she?" Dannie cringed as the exuberant girl ran up to her.

"Yep." KC nodded seriously. "You comes now."

"What if I'm not ready for my bath just yet?" Dannie questioned.

"You comes." KC glared at Dannie, stomping her foot on the ground. "Mommy says."

"Maybe I need to rethink this move," Dannie grumbled.

"Go on. You need a bath." Leevie shoved her lover, trying to encourage her to stand.

"I'll just bet that smartie rancher is back there laughing her fool head off 'bout sending this pipsqueak out to tell me what to do."

Leevie laughed. "Only way you're going to find out is to go back there."

KC tugged on the reluctant woman's shirt. "Comes on, Auntie Dannie. Watuh goin' git co'd."

Dannie grudgingly stood up and offered her good arm to Leevie, helping her to her feet. "Don't know about this," she grumbled as she let KC tug her in the direction of the back porch. "Next she's gonna be wanting to wash my back."

KC grinned. "Me he'ps. Me wike ta take baff. Cha-wie wikes baff too. But he spwashes too much. Gits watuhs ev'ywhe-uh."

Jennifer joined Jesse who was standing in front of the house, looking toward the sunset. "What are you looking at?"

Jesse wrapped her arm around her wife's waist, pulling her close. "Those clouds look different." She pointed to thick band of smoke clouds to the west. "They're not as dark as before."

"You think the fire's burning out?"

Jesse smiled. "I'm thinking there's rain coming. Air is damp, I can smell it."

"Thank goodness." Jennifer leaned into Jesse's embrace. She had long since tired of the acrid stench that hung in the air and irritated her throat. And of the soot and ash that persistently fell from the sky.

"Time we thought about going home, darlin'," Jesse said softly.

"Dannie's going into town tomorrow to see if she can find someone to buy the house and barn. Leevie figures she won't have any problem since houses are in such short supply. She said they should be ready to leave the day after. They don't have much to pack since they're not planning on bringing the furniture. They won't have any use for it in Sweetwater."

"We don't have to wait for them," Jesse offered.

"Do you mind if we do?" Jennifer turned her head to look into her wife's eyes. "You're still having trouble breathing, and I'd feel better—"

Jesse kissed Jennifer. "It's okay." She smiled when their lips parted.

"It is?"

"Sure. Another day or two won't make much difference. But I ain't riding in the back of that damn wagon."

"Wouldn't ask you to."

"Good." Jesse tightened her hold on Jennifer. "Maybe this time, we can remember to deliver Ed's package."

Jennifer laughed. "I can't believe we rode right through Philipsburg and never even thought of that."

"Seems we had more important matters to think about."

"I suppose you're right." Jennifer smiled. "Think we should go inside and save them from the young 'uns?"

"Nah. KC will come get us if Dannie starts to be a problem." Before Jennifer could correct her, Jesse resumed their kiss.

"Did you find a buyer?" Leevie asked when Dannie walked into the house. She and Jennifer were sitting on the settee enjoying a cup of coffee while Jesse played on the floor with the children.

Dannie smiled. "Sure did. Mr. Sullivan, at the Miners Hall, was mighty happy to hear I was selling. Seems he's been wanting to bring his wife here, but she refused to come 'til he had a decent house for her."

"How much do we still owe the bank?"

Dannie's smile widened. "Sullivan paid enough for the house and furniture to pay off the bank."

Leevie hurried across the room to hug her lover. "That's wonderful, Dannie."

"Shoulda sold this place before. Didn't realize how much demand there was for good houses. Seems Granite has grown out of available space for such as this one."

"I'm just happy we found a buyer, and we can pay off the bank."

"And we got some left over." Dannie lowered her voice. "Not much, but I was thinking you might want to take Jesse and Jennifer out to supper tonight. Maybe go to one of them fancy places in town you always wanted to try."

Leevie smiled. "I'd like that."

CHAPTER FIFTEEN

It took more than a week for Dannie's team of horses to pull the big freight wagon the distance from Granite to Sweetwater. Leevie rode beside Dannie on the wagon's high seat, while Jesse and Jennifer rode alongside on Dusty and Blaze. As much as riding tired her damaged leg, Jennifer had quickly discovered that being jostled about in the back of the heavy wagon as it bounced along the rutted road was much worse on her entire body. However, that didn't seem to bother KC and Charley, who spent most of the trip playing in the back of the wagon, empty except for the packs Boy would normally have carried and the few personal items Dannie and Leevie were bringing to Sweetwater.

Ed was sweeping off the front porch of the mercantile when the wagon and horses came into view as they made the turn around the Silver Slipper. He stopped his chore and rested the broom against the side of the building. "Jesse and Jennifer are back," he called into the store where Billie was stocking canned goods from the morning's delivery. "They ain't alone."

"Who'd they bring home this time?" Billie stepped out onto the porch. "That's a big wagon. You could sure use one of those around here."

"Sure could."

"Where are KC and Charley?"

"Don't see 'em. You best go get Ruthie." Ed stepped off the porch to walk to the Slipper, while Billie hurried across the street to the sewing shop to tell his wife of their friends' return.

"Afternoon, Ed," Jesse greeted as he approached.

"Good to see you back." Ed went directly to where Blaze had stopped beside the hitching post. He reached up to help Jennifer dismount. "We've been worried about you," he told her.

"We've been worried about you, too." Jennifer gave the big man a hug before pulling her cane free from the scabbard. "It looked like the fire was blowing this way."

Billie and Ruthie joined them, a sleeping baby in her arms. "So you know about that."

Jennifer smiled as she limped over to peek at the infant. "He's so cute," she whispered to Ruthie.

"Hard to have missed the smoke and fire," Jesse answered Billie as she dismounted. "Looked to be a big one."

"It was. For a while we thought it would come right through town, then the wind changed and blew it south." When Billie saw the worried look cross the rancher's face, he quickly added, "Ranch is fine, Jesse, so are your folks. I rode out and checked on them yesterday."

Jesse smiled in relief. "Thanks, Billie."

"You leave your young 'uns in Granite?" Ed asked.

"Nope." Jesse stepped to the back of the wagon.

"Auntie Dannie, 'et us outta hewe!" KC shouted from inside the wagon bed.

Climbing down from the wagon seat, Dannie grumbled under her breath. Instead of responding to KC's plea, she turned and helped Leevie climb down. "Should let her stay in there," she muttered.

Leevie giggled, poking Dannie in the ribs. "Stop that."

"Like you to meet a couple of friends," Jesse told the others. "This is Leevie Temple and Dannie Northly. Leevie is Sweetwater's new schoolteacher, and Dannie is your new freight driver."

"What?" Ed and Billie asked together.

The door to the Slipper burst open, and Bette Mae rushed through it. "I thought I heard voices out here," she said excitedly as she hurried to the edge of the porch.

"Auntie Dannie," KC shouted. "We's waitin'."

Bette Mae looked around for the girl. "Where is ya hidin' my li'l angel?" she asked Jesse.

"We's hewe, 'Ette."

Bette Mae eased out past the porch railing and peered over the side of the wagon. Two smiling faces greeted her. "Well, I'll be. Whatcha doin' in there?"

"Waitin' for Auntie Dannie to 'et us out," KC replied indignantly.

Dannie rolled her eyes, then reached for the back section of the wagon. Jesse helped lift the removable section free and set it on the ground.

"Hi, 'Ette," KC waved to the older woman on the porch. "Auntie Dannie, catch me."

"KC, no!" Jennifer cried as her daughter leapt off the back of the wagon before Dannie could react.

Jesse snatched her daughter out of the air. "KC Branson, you have got to stop doing that," she scolded.

"Sowwy, Mommy. I fo'gets."

Ed and Billie laughed as the girl looked at her displeased mother with sad eyes and her lower lip poked out in a pout.

"KC, you need to start remembering." Dannie smirked at Jesse's attempt to remain serious as KC gazed up at her, and Jesse growled at the freight driver, "You ain't helping."

"I ain't tryin' to."

"Mommy, I go see 'Ette?" KC asked.

"Course ya can come see me, li'l angel," Bette Mae said from the top of the steps, her arms open wide.

Encouraged by Bette Mae, KC struggled to get free of her mother's hold. "'et me down."

"Nope. You can wait 'til I help your momma up those steps." KC breathed out a big sigh and crossed her arms in frustration. Jesse waited for more of a protest, but her daughter remained silent and stopped struggling.

Dannie laughed. "Looks like you got some taming to do yet on that one." Jesse glared at her.

"Thought you said these were your friends, Jesse," Billie teased.

Jesse smirked. "Leevie is. Dannie, I ain't so sure about."

"Oh, you two." Jennifer shook her head. "Leevie, I'm not so sure this was such a good idea. Having the two of them in the same town could lead to trouble." She grinned at her friend.

Leevie returned the grin. "You're right, Jennifer. I guess we'll just have to make sure Dannie stays busy hauling freight and Jesse stays busy out at the ranch."

"What's this about Sweetwater having a new schoolteacher?" Ed asked when the women stopped laughing.

"And a new freight driver?" Billie added.

"Why don't we go inside and sit down?" Jesse suggested.

"That's a good idea, sweetheart." Jennifer wrapped her arm around Jesse's. "I could use something cold to drink, and I'm sure everyone else can, too."

"Well, what are we waiting for?" Dannie wrapped an arm around Leevie's waist and guided her toward the steps.

"Mommy!"

Everyone stopped and turned toward the sound of the new voice. Charley was sitting in the wagon, his arms stretched out and a look of annoyance on his face. "Up!"

Everyone turned and looked at KC, who was staring at her brother as if he had just grown a second head. "He talked," she said incredulously.

"Uh, oh," Jennifer whispered.

Dusty and Blaze, followed by Boy, walked through the gate and started down the slope to the ranch house. It was about an hour before sunset, and there was still plenty of light for the riders to see the damage the forest fire had left behind. To the east and south, dark slashes cut through the otherwise green forest and across the grasslands, stopping only when they reached the Sweetwater River. The fire had come close to the ranch buildings but skirted past, although there were patches of burnt ground scattered throughout.

"Jesse, why is some of the ground burned but not other sections?"

"Most likely, embers being blown in front of the main fire lit those areas up. They burned out before doing much damage. Least they didn't set any of the buildings on fire," Jesse said. Even though Billie had assured them the ranch had been untouched, she was relieved to see the proof with her own eyes.

"I'm so glad," Jennifer sighed. "I don't think I could have stood to see another house burned." Even with all the time that had passed since they'd returned from a trip and found their first home in ruins, she still shivered whenever she thought about it.

"Looks like Pop brought the cattle in," Jesse said. Their small herd was packed inside the corral. "Good thing we don't have any more than we do." She wondered how long the fencing would hold the crowded animals. "Best let them out soon."

"So much of the grassland burned, Jesse." Jennifer was looking beyond the ranch yard to the scorched hills where the cattle normally grazed. "How will we feed them?"

Jesse looked up into the sky where storm clouds had been building all day. "Soon as that lets loose," she smiled, "new grass will start sprouting up. In the meantime, I'm guessing Poppa has already talked to some of the other ranchers about buying hay."

"Speaking of them, where are your folks?" Jennifer turned her gaze toward the ranch buildings. "I don't see them."

"Dewe Gwumps." KC pointed as her grandfather walked out from behind the house. "Gwumps!" she shouted. "Gwumps, we's home."

Stanley Branson turned when he heard his granddaughter calling to him. "Marie," he called back to the garden where his wife was working. "Marie, they're back."

Jesse nudged Dusty into a trot, and Blaze immediately fell into step. By the time the horses reached the house, KC was already trying to scoot out of the saddle to greet her grandparents.

Jesse tightened her hold on the squirming girl. "Whoa there, Sunshine."

"Hi, Gwumps." KC waved, smiling happily. "Hi, Gwamma."

Marie hurried toward her daughters. "I was just saying to Stanley that I was hoping you'd be home tonight, and here you are." She reached up for KC, and Jesse passed her down. "You come give me a big hug," she said, wrapping her granddaughter in her arms. "I've missed you so much." KC giggled at her grandmother's attention.

Jesse slid out of the saddle and walked over to Blaze.

"You okay?" Stanley asked.

"We're fine, Poppa," Jesse said, helping Jennifer to the ground, then removing Charley from the carry sack on her back. She handed the baby to his grandfather. "Tell Grumps all about your trip." Jesse smirked when her father glared at her use of the nickname. "You have any problems with the herd?"

"Nope." Stanley smiled when Charley wrapped his arms around his neck and hugged him. "Billie came out and helped me round them up. Good thing we didn't move them into the high meadows," he admitted to his daughter. "Fire went through all of those."

Jesse looked to the east where the mountain meadows were located. "Guess that explains the knot in my gut whenever you said we needed to move them."

"You must be tired," Marie told Jennifer. "I bet you're hungry, too. I was just pulling up some carrots to put in the stew I have simmering."

"Yep." KC nodded. "I eats."

"And what about Charley?" Marie asked her granddaughter.

KC frowned. "He talks," she exclaimed in annoyance.

"Charley talked?"

"He said his first words today," Jennifer told Marie.

Jesse laughed. "KC hasn't quite gotten used to the idea." She smiled at Jennifer. "Go inside, darlin'. I'll be in as soon as I take care of the horses and get things unpacked."

"Don't worry about bringing any of that stuff in tonight, Jesse. We can make do without until tomorrow."

"All right," Jesse agreed, happy she didn't have to unload the heavy packs until the morning. "Go on," she said, giving her wife a quick kiss on the forehead. "I won't be long."

Jennifer waited until Jesse and Stanley walked away, leading the horses to the barn.

"Good trip?" Marie asked.

"Oh, yes." Jennifer smiled at her mother-in-law. "We have a lot to tell you. There's going to be a few more changes around here, besides Charley starting to speak for himself."

EPILOGUE

Jesse sat on the porch steps watching KC pick wildflowers that had sprouted in one of the burned patches close to the barn. They had been home almost a month, and the scorched ground was covered with new life after a series of rainstorms followed by sunny days.

"'ook, Mommy," KC cried excitedly as she ran across the yard, her fist full of bright purplish-red flowers. "What dis caw-ed?" she asked when she pulled to a stop in front of her mother.

"Those, Sunshine," Jesse said, lifting the girl into her lap, "are called fireweed. You know why?"

"Nope."

"Because after there's a fire and the rains come, they're the flowers that usually come up first. When you see them blooming, you know the land is on the mend."

"Dey pwetty."

"They sure are."

"Momma wike?"

"She sure will." Jesse caught the movement of a rider coming over the top of the hillock and turned her head toward the ranch gate. She recognized the horse as one the livery in town offered for hire, but she didn't recognize the rider.

"Who dat?" KC asked when she looked to see what had drawn her mother's attention.

"Don't know. Guess we'll just have to wait until they get here." Jesse stood and mounted the steps to the porch. She placed KC in one of the chairs there. "Stay put, okay?"

"Okay."

Jesse stepped back to the edge of the porch to greet the stranger. She nodded a greeting when the man rode up. "Afternoon."

"Afternoon," the man said nervously. "I'm looking for Jesse Branson. I was told I could find her here."

"I'm Jesse. Who are you?"

"Name is Todd Evans. My sister was Catherine Evans. You probably knew her by her married name of Williams."

Jesse's heart fell, and it was all she could do not to show the jumble of emotions she was feeling. "What's your business?" she asked through clenched teeth.

"I was told in Bannack that my sister's child was with you."

"You ain't taking her," Jesse snarled. "We've got a paper signed by Judge Henry saying she's ours."

"Mommy?" Hearing the distress in her mother's voice, KC climbed down from the chair and hugged Jesse's leg.

Jesse placed her hand protectively on her daughter's head. "It's okay, Sunshine," she told the frightened girl, keeping her eyes on the stranger.

Evans looked affectionately at KC. "She favors my sis," he said, smiling at some long forgotten memories before raising his eyes to look at Jesse. "You don't need to be worrying about me taking her. Folks in Bannack told me what happened and how you took the baby in as your own. I'm obliged. Just wanted to see her. She's…" He shrugged. "Guess you could say she's all that's left of my sis."

KC raised her hands above her head. "Mommy, up."

Her fears calmed by the man's assurances, Jesse relaxed and lifted her daughter into her arms.

"Sis would be grateful she has loving folks looking out for her."

"She is loved, Mr. Evans." Jesse smiled when KC wrapped her arms around her neck and kissed her. "Would you like to sit a spell?" Jesse asked. "We've got some coffee warming on the stove."

"Wish I had the time, but I've got a ticket on the next stage west, and I need to be getting back to Sweetwater."

"Mommy, who dat?" KC whispered in Jesse's ear.

"That's Mr. Evans. He's your uncle."

KC tilted her head to the side, studying the man. She scrunched her nose up and whispered, "He no 'ook wike Momma."

Jesse chuckled when Evans looked at her quizzically. "Sorry, the only uncle she knows is my wife's brother. They favor each other. You don't look much like him."

"I bet I don't." Evans laughed, pushing his hat back on his head. "I must say I'm surprised to find her looking so healthy."

"Why's that?"

"Seems I remember my sis writing that she was a sickly baby. They didn't think she'd make it through the first year."

"You must know how old she is then," Jennifer said hopefully, pushing open the screen door to step out on the porch carrying Charley. She had been inside preparing supper when she heard Jesse talking to someone. Not recognizing the voice, she had stood just inside the door listening to the conversation. "And her given name."

"This is my wife, Jennifer," Jesse said proudly when Jennifer joined her. "And our son, Charley."

"Pleasure, ma'am." Evans tapped the brim of his hat in salute. "But don't you know?" he responded to Jennifer's questions.

"No. When we found her, there was nothing that said. No one in Bannack knew much about your sister or husband and even less about KC."

"KC?"

"We found a wallet with the names Kenneth and Catherine Williams," Jesse explained. "We figured them to be her folks. Jennifer thought it was fitting to name her after them."

"That's a nice gesture," Evans said. "Well, let me think..." He leaned back in the saddle, swinging a leg over the horse's neck to rest it across the saddle. "Seems I got a letter saying sis had given birth just before the end of spring. Though I don't recall her saying what they named the baby."

"Are you sure?"

"Best as I can recollect. Can't remember her saying the exact day, either, if that's what you're wanting to know."

"It would be nice, but what you remembered helps." Jennifer leaned against Jesse. Disappointed that KC's uncle couldn't tell them more, still they now knew their daughter was a few months older than they had guessed.

"I'd best be getting back." Evans swung his leg back over the horse's neck, slipping his boot into the stirrup.

Jesse stepped off the porch, lifting KC up to sit on her shoulders. "Thank you." She offered a hand to Evans. "You're welcome any time. I'm sure when she's a bit older, KC would like to know about your sister."

Evans shook Jesse's hand. "Doubt I'll be back through these parts. I'm headed for the Oregon Territory. If things don't work out there, I'll be trying my luck in California. Besides, you're her family now." He nodded goodbye to Jennifer. "You're a lucky woman, Jesse Branson. There's lots of folks would feel blessed to be standing in your place. Best you never forget it." He tapped the sides of the horse and pulled the reins to turn him away from the house.

"I won't." Jesse watched the man ride away. When he had disappeared over the hillock, she went back to the porch and up the steps where she set KC down beside Jennifer.

"Jesse?" Jennifer asked when her wife marched past her.

"Something I've been meaning to do." Jesse stopped to hold the screen door open for Jennifer before walking across the room and up the stairs.

"Jesse?"

"Be right back," Jesse called down the stairs.

Jennifer didn't have to wait long before Jesse came back down the stairs carrying a framed piece of glass. She watched as Jesse stopped at the foot of the stairs and studied the wall in front of her.

Jesse held the frame up to the wall, her arms stretched out as far as they could go and her back arched back away from the wall to add to the distance her eyes had to look. She moved the frame a little to the left. Then back to the right. Then up a bit. She smiled and nodded, then set the frame on the floor and leaned it against the wall. "I'll be right back. Don't touch that," she told Jennifer. "And don't move." Then she walked through the kitchen and out the back door.

"Whe-uh Mommy go?" KC asked.

"I don't know."

"I goes 'ook fo' hewe?"

"Better not. She said to stay here."

Just then the back door opened, and Jesse entered, carrying a hammer and with a nail sticking out from between her lips. She stopped in front of the frame. Removing the nail from her lips, she pounded it into the wall, then lifted the frame and hung it on the nail.

Jennifer walked over to stand beside her grinning wife. "Mind letting me know what you're doing?"

"Had Ed make that up for me that last time I was in town. Been trying to decide where to hang it. I wanted the perfect place and that's it. Every time I come downstairs, I'll see it. Every time I walk from the kitchen into the sitting room, or from here into the kitchen, I'll see it. It'll remind me what's most important to me." Jesse wrapped her arms around Jennifer, holding her wife in front of her and turning her in the direction of the wall. "Like Evans said, never forget. I never intend to," she said, resting her head against her wife's.

Jennifer sighed, tears filling her eyes. Neatly framed under the glass were three pieces of paper, each having meaning to the women that no words could ever express. "Sweetheart, it's beautiful."

"I'm glad you like it, darlin'."

KC tugged on Jesse's pant leg. "Mommy, what dat?"

Jesse bent down and lifted the girl into her arms. "Well, Sunshine," she said as she held KC so she could see. She pointed to a piece of paper under the glass. "That says that I belong to your momma." It was the marriage certificate Mayor Perkins had presented to them the night of their wedding. Jesse pointed to KC's adoption papers. "And this says you belong to Momma and me. And this one," she pointed to the third piece of paper protected by the glass, "says that Charley belongs to Momma and me."

Jennifer slipped her arm around her wife's waist. "And all of them together say that we're a family. And that's the most valuable possession we'll ever have."

"That it is." Jesse leaned in for a kiss. "That it is."

Mickey was born and raised in Southern California. She has lived in New Mexico and Washington state and, for the past several years, in Western Montana. A lifelong history and nature enthusiast, Mickey has explored many of the locations she uses in her stories. She is also a photographer and enjoys recording the natural beauty of Montana as well as documenting the remnants of life in the frontier.

Mickey has plans for several more books and looks forward to the day she can spend all her time writing. Visit Mickey's website at mickeyminner.com

Breinigsville, PA USA
27 May 2010
238835BV00003B/65/P